Heavens *to* Betsy

Norma Eaton

Paperback-Press
an imprint of A & S Publishing
A & S Holmes, Inc.

ISBN: 1-945669-04-7
ISBN-13: 978-1-945669-04-0

DEDICATION

In memory of my precious sister, Donna, who brought joy and love to all who knew her; but who left to be with the Lord much too soon. I take comfort in knowing she is one of God's special angels just as she was our special angel here on earth. She is always in our hearts, for love never dies.

1 Corinthians, 13:13: *And now these three remain: faith, hope and love. But the greatest of these is love.*

ACKNOWLEDGMENTS

To my husband Gary and my daughters Lynn and Lori, you have made my life complete. God blessed me with a wonderful family and great friends. Thank you all for your love and encouragement.

.

CHAPTER ONE

It really shouldn't have come to any great surprise to Kara that Betsy died. Her friends and family had warned her it could happen anytime, but Kara wouldn't listen to such talk. Sure Betsy was old and not in the greatest shape, but she amazed everyone how well she moved along for her advanced age. To some her demise would be considered a blessing, but to Kara it couldn't have happened at a worse time. Not that *any* time would be a *good* time to die. Kara stared at Betsy in stunned dismay expecting one last cough or whine, but there was no response. Not even a wheeze.

"Well, old gal." Kara sighed. "I guess you're definitely dead—*again!*" Kara backed off and gave Betsy a swift kick in the tire. "You traitor! So close...just a few blocks from the church." Her shoulders sagged as she pulled a tissue out of her purse and dabbed at the perspiration beaded across her forehead. With only fifteen minutes to get to her best friend's wedding, she would have to run and run fast.

She should have traded old Betsy off for a new car long ago, but the old Buick was like family to her and as frustrating as the car could be, she just couldn't part with it. Gramps had given it to her before he died and, no, she could never get rid of Betsy.

"Kara Peters, you are nuts," she said out loud, taking off with all the gusto of a hundred-yard dash. "How refreshing. Running in high heels in August." She tried to picture herself in

Nome, Alaska, instead of Peoria Heights, Illinois. It didn't work. With sweaty hands she fumbled with her cell phone and dialed her brother's friend Jack to come to her rescue. He worked for a towing company and was not too receptive to the idea of "borrowing" his boss's tow truck again.

"Kara, I'm running out of excuses why I need to use the tow, free gratis, that is."

"You have to eat lunch, don't you?"

"Lunch," he repeated blandly. "How many people do you know who borrow a tow truck to go to lunch?"

"Please Jack. I'm desperate. I have someone's drive blocked." By now she was panting so hard, she could barely speak.

"Are you running?"

"A little, but I made it. I'm at the church…"

"You know you should not be exerting yourself. The doctors say you—"

"I'm okay, Jack. I know my limitations. Betsy is on Glen a couple blocks from Prospect. Tow the car to the side entrance of the church. You'll have the tow truck back at work before you know it. I'll fix the car myself. Bring an ice pick, about five inches of copper wire and needle-nose pliers."

"An ice pick?"

"Yes, I know exactly what's wrong with it."

"So do I," he butt in. "It needs the ashtray jacked up and a new car run under it."

"Side entrance, Jack. I owe you one."

"One? Ha! More like a hundred and one. I promised your brother Paul to look after you when you moved back to Peoria, I didn't promise to raise you."

"Gotta hang up. I'm walking into the church. Love you!"

"Yeah, yeah, yeah, love you too."

Still breathing hard from her heated sprint, Kara got to her seat just seconds before the Wedding March boomed through the air. She dabbed at her misty eyes as she watched her very dear friends, Barb and John, exchange vows before a multitude of well-wishers who had come to witness the joyous occasion.

Weddings always made her cry, but then so did car trouble three times in one week. Her mind snapped back to the present when the preacher stated, "I now pronounce you man and wife. You may kiss the bride."

As the organ music swelled, a smile beamed across Kara's face watching the happy couple run down the aisle to take their place in the reception line just outside the church. Her eyes glanced briefly to the best man and Barb's sister who served as maid of honor then darted back to the best man. He looked familiar but she couldn't place where she had seen him. He was certainly a handsome brute. His dark features and perfectly groomed hair made her think of Prince Charming. Hair. Hers must be a mess! She fluffed the sides with her fingers. This was one time she was thankful for her naturally wavy hair. The humidity only tightened the short blond curls.

She rose with the rest of her row and filed out toward the wedding party to congratulate them. As she approached the bride, a loud bang was heard. All heads turned toward a rattling tow truck, dragging an old Buick behind, sputter to a stop right in front of the church.

"I told him the SIDE entrance," she said under her breath, embarrassed for the disturbance. She raised her arm to catch Jack's attention to wave him on. Her shoulders dropped knowing he had not seen her motion. How could he? The diesel smoke was thicker than pea soup.

Wanting to waste no time getting through the reception line to strangle Jack, she quickly gave Barb a big hug telling her what a beautiful bride she made. Barb coughed and waved at smoke filling the air. "Is that your car?" she whispered. Kara could only shrug her shoulders and whisper, "I'm sorry." She hurriedly shook John's hand, then peered out toward the street again.

"Surely I get more than a handshake," John teased, also fanning the smoke out of his face. "After all, I'm taking Barb off your hands for a couple of weeks."

"Yeah, sure," Kara said distractedly, still trying to see what Jack was doing. "I hope you and Barb have a long and happy life together." With that she closed her eyes, turned, and kissed him squarely on the mouth. Her immediate thought was, when did John grow so tall? Her second thought was, who the heck is this? Her eyes flew open to see pale blue ones staring back at her. John's eyes were brown. "Ohhhh, good grief! I kissed the wrong man!"

"Aww," the just-kissed man returned lightly. "And I was about to ask if it was as good for you as it was for me."

Barb couldn't help but giggle at Kara's predicament, and John commented dryly, "So you want the best man here to have a long and happy life with *my* wife?"

"No." Kara felt her cheeks burn. "I mean…oh, I'm so sorry."

"Don't be sorry on my part," the dark-haired man said, still smiling down at her.

"It's just that I…uh…mmm, left the gift in my car and…" She stopped, smiled and drew a deep breath. She wasn't sounding convincing at all. "Would you believe the heat has dried up my brain?"

John and Barb nodded in agreement and laughed, but the best man just continued smiling down at her.

Kara slowly backed away. "So…I guess I'll see you at the reception. It's been, well…swell." She laughed nervously and as soon as she was out of their sight ran around to the side of the church, motioning Jack to follow.

How could she have kissed the wrong man? "Look up 'klutz' in the dictionary," she mumbled to no one in particular. "My picture is there." She could still smell the 'wrong' man's aftershave.

"I told you the SIDE, Jack," she scolded as he let her car down to the ground.

Jack jumped out of the truck, wiped the sweat from his neck and handed her the tools she had requested.

"Kara, your face is red as fire. I knew you were over-doing it. If anything happens to you under my watch…"

"Jack! Stop it. I'm fine. It's just the heat."

The August sun was bearing down mercilessly and Kara needed to work fast before it melted her to a puddle. She lifted the hood on the Buick and began to carefully poke at one of the connections with the ice pick.

Jack handed her the remains of his soft drink. "Want the rest of my lunch?"

Kara huffed. "If you think giving me the last swallow of your warm Coke is going to make up for parking this noisy tow truck right in front of the church door with everyone trying to exchange greetings while choking on diesel smoke—"

"Hey, I'm here, ain't I?" He leaned against the rusty fender of the truck while she clamped one end of the copper wire with the pliers. "Are you drinking plenty of liquids?"

She raised up and slammed the hood down, then turned to Jack. "Yes, Mother, I'm drinking water, eating right, resting, explaining myself to—"

"Okay, you don't have to get huffy."

"Sorry. I'm being rude. Thanks for your help, but Jack?"

"Yeah?"

"I've lived with this heart thing all my life. I know what I can and cannot do. God is with me always. I'll be fine."

She got in behind the wheel and turned the ignition. With just a brief hesitation, the old Buick purred to a start. She smiled, turned it off and got out.

"Old Betsy here and I go back a long way. I don't know what I'd do without her."

"I hate to break the news, but it's not a 'her'. It's a bucket of bolts...in the purist form." He looked at her and shook his head in amazement. "I don't know how you do it."

"Do what?"

"Work on your car without even getting dirty."

She looked down at her spotless yellow dress and laughed reminiscently. "I didn't always look this tidy when I worked for my brother in his service station."

"I remember. Could hardly see you for the grime."

"Thanks for the compliment. In those days, I hadn't spent much on clothes. I wouldn't dare get this dress dirty. The money I spent on it represents my living room carpet, which will have to wait a few weeks longer. The contractor who worked on the barn cost quite a bit but was worth it. He did a fantastic job on turning it into a dormitory. 'Kids Haven' will one day be the place Gramps envisioned while he was able to do a lot of the work himself. I'm determined to carry out his wishes. There are a lot of kids in this world who need love and a safe, Godly place to come to."

Jack moaned. "You're going to be working on that old farm he left you forever. Why don't you think about a nice, calm hobby like knitting?"

"Why don't you shut up," she teased, kissing him on the cheek. "Stop grumbling and get out of here so I can get to the reception." Adding, "Again, thanks and I owe you. Come over sometime and I'll make dinner."

"Forget it." He laughed. "I've seen your kitchen."

CHAPTER TWO

The following week passed rather quickly with all the work Kara had to do, mostly sanding and painting inside the barn, getting Kids Haven completed. Gramps had already applied for the license and permit to house needy children and she wanted to be ready for the official inspection next month.

Her house was still a disaster, but that wasn't as important as getting the dormitory in tip top shape. Staining the woodwork was tedious and the odor left her breathless occasionally, but she made it without too many complications. She only had to use her portable oxygen once and that was her own fault for over-doing it.

When Gramps left the family this farm he knew *she* would finish what he started. Her family thought it was too much for her to take on but she assured them it was God's will. Her brother Paul was a little harder to convince, but finally he came around if she allowed his best friend Jack to 'watch over her' since he couldn't leave Joliet.

He had his service station to run. When she agreed to Paul's dictate she never knew Jack would be attached to her hip most of the time. They all grew up together and she loved Jack like a brother, but if he wasn't with her, he was calling to check on her. She appreciated his friendship and thanked God for his concern, but he worried a little too much. Rheumatic heart disease scared him more than it scared her.

Except for the faint scratching of a ballpoint pen across the report pad, the only sound in the room was an occasional yawn as her body stretched, defying caffeine's reputation for keeping one alert, creative and energetic. Well, she thought, this certainly wasn't the first morning she had set her alarm for three o'clock to work on the never-ending stack of paperwork she had inherited with her position as Case Worker for the Illinois Department of Children and Family Services, and it probably wouldn't be the last.

Thank God it was Friday, she mumbled to herself as she laid the pen down and slumped back against the kitchen chair, sipping the strong, black coffee. Her eyes slowly appraised the unorganized debris in the room. Boxes of unpacked dishes and pans, sacks of canned goods, soap powder and other kitchen essentials sat staring back at her. When would she ever find the time to get started on remodeling the house? What a heck of a friend Barb turned out to be. Running off on her honeymoon just when the case load took a giant leap.

A grin formed easily across her face as she thought about the wedding last Sunday. Barb made a beautiful bride and John was nervously handsome in his tux. Kara sighed reflectively and rose to pour herself another cup of coffee, feeling her face flush as she recalled her stupid blunder of kissing the wrong man. After the reception she had drifted outside the church to a quiet spot beneath a giant weeping willow tree, searching for a cool breeze.

"Hello." There he was; his voice deep and rather husky.

"Hello, yourself." She had tried to sound casual. "Hot enough for you?"

Man! She couldn't believe she asked that stupid question. Why couldn't she ever invent something sophisticated to say at times like that...like...like... "This weather reminds me of the summer I spent in the Caribbean." But noooo, she had to ask, "Hot enough for you?", when they were both melting down into their shoes.

Her reminiscing was suddenly interrupted by a whine at the door. Kara smiled as she let in Pooch, a giant St. Bernard that befriended her the first day she moved in. She had tried to find his owner, but to no avail, and now Pooch was part of her family along with Smokey, her gray cat of questionable origin, who moved with Kara from Joliet nearly six months ago.

"Hey, Pooch, what's the matter? Did I wake you?" Kara scratched the top of his head.

She opened the door wide enough for the large dog to enter, and Smokey slithered past them like a streak and hopped onto the chair Kara had just vacated.

"You too?" She laughed as Pooch wiggled his hindquarters, nearly knocking her down as he excitedly greeted her. "Okay, okay," she called out. "Just a small snack then back out you go. This place is a big enough mess without you guys knocking things over." She tried to sound stern, but 'stern' was never one of her strong suits.

She took what was left of a carton of ice-cream from the freezer compartment of her relic refrigerator. Frost had nearly sealed the tiny space closed and she had to tear the carton to get it loose. "When we get rich," she promised her two guests, "we are going to have a big frost-free, side-by-side refrigerator-freezer and all the ice-cream we want!" She frantically searched through a couple grocery sacks until she found the paper plates, then divided the ice-cream between the three of them.

The pets scrambled forward and Kara held the plates up high. "Oh, no. Pray first."

The two animals obediently bowed their heads as Kara thanked God for all he has done for them.

"Good boys." She placed their plates on the floor and petted each of them. "I'm so amazed how quickly you learned how to pray. It only took me, what? Less than a month and you had it down pat." She smiled broadly. "You are two smart dudes, you know that? Too bad humans can't learn to pray that fast."

Pooch's portion was immediately inhaled and Smokey daintily licked at hers, glaring at Pooch between each lick defying him to even LOOK like he wanted a bite.

"Mmmm, this is good. I'm glad you dropped in. I needed a cool break." It was one of those hot August nights when you couldn't buy a breeze.

"Do you want to hear about this guy I met at the wedding?" The pets' ears perked hearing her voice. "He was good looking…great looking, in fact. Not too tall, not too short, probably…umm six feet, early thirties, neat as a pin, looking fresh as a daisy. Probably didn't even know how to sweat." She giggled. "He had a nice voice…" She cleared her throat. "Oh, did I tell you I kissed him?" Pooch raised his head. "Well, it was an accident." She noted the dog's blank stare. "You had to be there." She took another bite of ice-cream. "He was certainly polite considering that stupid kiss thing. He just took my hand and introduced himself. Kevin something."

She finished her ice-cream. "His hand was surprisingly cool, like a refreshing spray off the ocean on a cool night." She laughed at herself again. What would she know about an ocean spray? The only body of water she was familiar with was the Illinois River and who would want a 'spray' from that?"

"It's a good thing you weren't there, Pooch. You would have been ashamed of me. I acted so ignorant. Like my brain went north for the summer. I don't think I said two intelligent words in a row from the time I…well, you know…did that kiss thing." She breathed in noisily. "Anyway, I just got into my hot Buick and came home." She rose. "And that's the end of that story."

Pooch and Smokey continued staring at her. "Okay, I know. I don't need to be thinking about him. I forgot him already. Don't worry." That wasn't totally true. He was hard to forget, but she had to.

She gathered up their dirty plates and stuffed them into the garbage sack in the cabinet beneath the sink, noting a small leak in the pipe leading to the faucet.

The floor of the cabinet was moist where it had dripped and soaked into the garbage sack. "Oh, no!" She searched through a box for a pie pan to place under the drip. She would have to pick up a new fitting on her way home from work.

"Come on, guys. Party's over. Out you go. I've got to get ready."

She shooed them out the door, giving Pooch a friendly pat on the rump, then yawned and ran her fingers through the mat of damp curls at her nape. As she walked toward the bathroom to take her morning shower, she vowed out loud, "When I'm filthy rich, another thing I'm going to have is an air conditioner that will frost my socks off!" Something made her form a mental picture of her 'wrong man' acquaintance from the wedding, lying peacefully asleep under a blanket while cool blasts of air circulated around his dark, perfectly groomed hair. "Lucky creep." She mentally slapped herself. There she was thinking about him again!

She snapped on the light in the bathroom, immediately shading her eyes from the glaring bare bulb in the ceiling. A globe for the light fixture also went on her 'when I get filthy rich' list. She sighed. She needed so many things for the house but what money Gramps left was only to be used to finish getting "Kids Haven" up and running before…well before time ran out. God had granted her many more years than anticipated and she was not going to waste them.

Dropping her short nightgown into the clothes hamper, she absently pulled another strip of curling wallpaper off the wall and tossed it into the wastebasket before stepping into the shower. She adjusted the water temperature and burst into her best rendition of "Oh What a Beautiful Morning" and ended with "Amazing Grace."

She was still humming as she finished dressing in a cool blue cotton blouse and matching skirt. After putting out fresh water and food for her sleeping roommates on the porch, she grabbed her briefcase and sauntered out to her car, ready to face whatever the day would bring.

The old Buick wended its way along Big Hollow Road avoiding as many pot holes as possible, until it reached the main route which led to the city. Kara rolled down the window to let the breeze in and switched on the radio which refused to come to life until she tapped the dash with the palm of her hand in the secret, strategic spot. She smiled. If she wanted the radio to come on, it wouldn't by itself, but it would come on automatically on its own at top volume at inopportune times. And it only worked on one station—oldies, but goodies. When she rode with Gramps as a kid, she thought it was funny, and she guessed it still was…a little…if you liked the old songs, especially Elvis Presley.

She arrived at her office a short time later and immediately swung into action. Though the day was a hectic one, it went better than most and Kara was pleased with her accomplishments, smiling happily as she pulled into her driveway that afternoon. Her two exuberant roomies rounded the house giving her a welcome anyone would be proud of.

There seemed to be a third voice in the crowd. Heard, but not seen. Kara cautiously opened the car door to carefully explore where the other bark was coming from. There before her was a black and tan dachshund, looking about a dog and a half long and a half a dog high.

Kara laid her head back on the seat and prayed. "Dear God, please let him belong to the neighbor." She looked down at him again. His front paws were resting at the edge of the floorboard, his tail wagging so fast it looked like a propeller. He let out a heart rendering whimper and Kara instinctively petted his head. "You *are* kind of cute...in a homely sort of way."

She then straightened. "Okay, let's find out who you belong to." As she walked toward the house, the pets tangled themselves with her legs every step of the way. She let herself in, cautioning her friends to stay outside and wait for her to bring them fresh water and food.

The little mutt hungrily woofed down a good portion of food before Kara could stop him, then pointed a finger at Pooch and Smokey. "Just because he doesn't know how to pray doesn't mean you can skip it." She tapped them on the head. "Pray first." They bowed and Kara said Grace. The little dog instinctively sat back on his haunches and watched until the other pets began to eat before he resumed his meal.

Kara shook her head slowly. The dachshund actually waited for the prayer to end. God works in mysterious ways. "Okay, you can stay the weekend, but come Monday morning I'm placing an ad in the paper." Smokey looked at her with disbelieving eyes. "I mean it. I can't afford room and board for every stray in the country!" Pooch let out a soft "woof".

"I don't need your pitiful comments. Just because you're a big old softie doesn't mean I am. Monday he's gone."

The big dog let out a louder "woof" and Kara just waived her hand and called out as she went into the house. "Not working, Pooch."

CHAPTER THREE

After finding a pair of old jeans and cutting the legs off to make shorts out of them, Kara stood before the open refrigerator door trying to decide on the leftover goulash or the contents in the orange bowl. Since she didn't exactly remember how long the orange bowl had been in there, she started to opt for the goulash, then decided to give eating another thought after she mowed her lawn. Tuesday's rain had given the grass a good two-inch boost.

She noticed one leg of her cut-offs was considerably longer than the other so she gave it a couple of whacks with the scissors. Now it was considerably shorter than the other. She shrugged and snipped off some loose threads from her tattered halter. "Who cares? No one's going to see me."

Grunting, she pulled the old push mower out from under the back porch and went about her chore with diligence, huffing and groaning through the yard. Boy, she thought, by the time the honeymooners get back, their yard is going to be a jungle. Chuckling, she said loudly as if her friends could hear her, "You creeps, lying around in some air-conditioned honeymoon suite...only kidding." She was actually tickled to death they finally tied the knot and escaped the hot rat race for a couple of weeks. They had planned the wedding three different times and each time some crisis in either Barb's or John's profession caused a postponement. Kara's predecessor's leaving was the cause the last time and Kara recalled, with amusement, Barb's frantic call begging her to move back to Peoria and take the position.

The timing had been right. The day care center where she had been working was being closed due to lack of funds and with Gramps passing, Kara knew she wanted to continue his work on the farm to finish the Haven for needy children. She and Barb had gone all through grade school together and had always remained friends even after Kara's family moved to Joliet. Barb was the sister Kara wished she had and she cherished that friendship. Being raised with four brothers, five counting Jack, didn't leave her much of a chance for 'girl talk' around home.

Kara gave the mower another healthy shove into a stubborn clump of grass and found herself envying Barb's marital status. Where did that thought come from? She was always glad to see happily married couples, but envy? Seems like ever since she met that man at the wedding, all kinds of crazy thoughts ran through her mind. Never before had she given a relationship with a man a second thought. She reminded herself that she could never marry or even have a relationship. It wouldn't be fair to him. Granted, God had given her more years than expected by the doctors and she felt so very blessed, but she had no guarantee how long she had on earth. She needed to be practical and get those foolish thoughts out of her head.

She finished the last swipe with the mower, wiped her sweaty forehead with the back of her arm and went straight to the refrigerator for a cold drink. While she sipped on her soda, the thought came to her that it would be a nice surprise to mow Barb and John's yard. It wouldn't be nearly as hard as her own because they had a riding mower and she knew where they kept the key to their utility shed.

The more she thought about it, the more the idea of riding around on their mower sounded like fun. Ever since she helped out at her brother's service station in Joliet, she had been fascinated by anything with a motor. She prided herself on being the only woman she knew who could overhaul an engine.

When she tossed her empty bottle in the trash sack beneath the sink, it dawned on her she had forgotten to get the fitting.

She emptied the pie pan and placed it back under the drip. That settled it. She would definitely mow Barb and John's lawn since their new house was on the way to the hardware store. Afterwards she could eat a couple of Coney dogs and pick up the fitting. She had wanted to get over to Barb's house before they came back anyway to put up the hanging planter she had made them as a coming home present.

She searched and found the decorator hook she purchased to hang the planter with, grabbed up the gift from the bare living room where she had made it and promised herself she would make time tomorrow to clean up all the jute fuzz and scraps left from her projects.

****

She drove slowly down the shady street, looking at all the beautiful houses. Barb had been so proud of her new home and Kara was thrilled for her to finally be able to move in. When she pulled up to the front of the split-level brick house, her mouth dropped open. The yard looked manicured. The hedge was trimmed as neat as an army crewcut. An edger had been skillfully used along the sidewalk leading to the front door and, as she stepped out of her car the smell of charcoal filtered to her nose.

Was the honeymoon over so soon? She smiled as she walked to their back yard, wondering if she would be intruding. Had she known they would be home, she would have dressed a little more appropriately.

As she rounded the side of the house, she saw a man squatting beside the riding mower, mumbling not-so-nice words to it. He had his back to her but she knew it was not John. She back-tracked a few steps, looking at the house again to make sure she had the right one, then stepped forward again.

"Hello there," she called politely, trying not to startle the stranger.

The man turned his dark head her way and she froze in her tracks. Even the scowl on his face couldn't hide his perfect features and the sensuous brows she had remembered. Not to mention the mesmerizing pale blue eyes that had haunted her for

15

a week. His full lips parted a fraction, but before he could speak, Kara yelled, "It's *you*!!"

"You're right as rain, lady. It IS me," he returned dryly, straightening his long lean frame to its full height.

Kara's heart thudded against her rib cage. He was wearing short boxer-type bathing trunks whose crease would slice meat and her first thought was, who would press a bathing suit? It certainly made her painfully aware of her crooked cut-offs and faded halter. Her gaze wandered back up to his cool expression. She knew it! He wasn't even sweating!

He eyed her up and down. "Do I know you?".

CHAPTER FOUR

"Uh...uh...you do...you do know me." All the little cute and clever things she had memorized to say if she ever saw him again vanished and she was talking like she had six tongues.

He walked closer, studying her face. She studied his bare chest, her eyes following the path of dark hair down until it disappeared into the snow white, crisp trunks. She dwelled momentarily on his two sculpted knees, then on down past his muscled calves to his feet standing perfectly straight in leather thongs. His toenails look like they had been manicured and buffed.

Her eyes snapped back to his face when she heard, "We've met before?"

"Yes." She was tempted to say, yes, I believe it was during my sabbatical in Hawaii, but instead, "Yes. Barb and John's wedding." She could tell it didn't ring a bell with him. "I'm Kara Peters." He slowly shook his head trying to recall. "Barb's friend...uh...who couldn't distinguish between the groom and best man."

"Oh, that was you?" His gaze quickly scanned her attire. "You look different."

Now was the time for another of those sophisticated replies like, with the mansion on fire, I was lucky to escape with my life, grabbing the scullery maid's clothes on my way out. All that came to mind was, "Yeah, well, I've always been known for my versatility. Comes in handy when I'm dodging bill collectors."

He obviously found that amusing and laughed out loud. She laughed with him. He was now standing very close and she had to tilt her head up slightly to enjoy the full view of his perfect teeth as his laughter settled into a grin. His brows even looked combed! She searched frantically for one speck of dirt or a blade of grass stuck to him. When SHE mowed the lawn, her feet always turned green. Oh, mercy! Her feet were green at this very minute sticking out of her old rubber thongs. Please, Lord, don't let him look at my feet!

"Your feet are green," he said matter-of-factly.

You had to do it, didn't you, Lord? "I *am* a mess. I just finished mowing my own lawn. In fact," she added, putting the hanging planter on the ground to give her arms a rest, "I just came over to mow Barb's lawn and hang this gift I made as a surprise, but I see the lawn's nearly finished." She pointed to the patio roof. "I'll just hang this and..." Her voice trailed to a whisper as she watched his gaze still going from her head to her green toes. "I'll be going along as soon as I..."

"*You* were going to ride that thing?" He pointed disgustedly at the little tractor.

"No, I was going to push it." She laughed, adding, "Of course, I was going to ride it. What have YOU been doing on it? Tap dancing?"

He laughed at her remark, his own sense of humor returning. "I might as well have been. I've been hours getting this much accomplished. Start, go, die, start, go, die. That's all it's done. I'm about to give up and leave the rest for John."

"Then I take it they're not back yet?" She looked toward the patio doors to see into the kitchen.

"No, they're still connubial blissing in Wisconsin Dells, I suppose."

"I didn't know. I thought I smelled charcoal."

"You do. I'm house sitting. I'm having my apartment repainted and needed a place to stay for a few days. John offered their place." He put his hands on his hips in an exasperated manner as he looked around. "What anyone wants a house for is beyond me. All this upkeep."

"Well, I'm sure they'll appreciate their yard mowed when they get back."

"Partially mowed," he corrected, pointing to the mower. "The little monster went directly to 'die' and refused to go through its 'start, go' mode."

"What seems to be its trouble, I wonder," she said interestedly as she walked over to the machine and turned its starter.

"Be careful! I'm not very good at playing homeowner and even worse at playing doctor."

She gave him a wary glance.

"I mean playing doctor in the literal sense." He grinned. "I don't want you to cut off any of those green toes."

She paid him no mind and studied the internal workings of the motor for a few seconds, then reached in and secured a small wire that was loosely connected. She climbed into the seat and started the motor without a grumble, giving in to the urge to cast her surprised acquaintance a smug glance as she motored past him, sitting regally tall and proud as she finished the lawn in record time.

After she put the tractor away and fastened the padlock in place, she sauntered playfully over to the patio where the tall, dark and handsome man sat sipping a cool drink and ending a call on his cell. He placed his phone on the table and raised his head to look at her. She bit her lip to keep from giggling and brushed her hands together. "Well, so much for that little task. Anything else you need me to do while I'm here?"

His somber look turned into a mischievous grin. "Yeah, I could think of a few things."

She raised one brow, cautioning, "Don't make me say a disparaging word, Mister, uh…"

"Michals, without the 'e'. Kevin Michals. That's M-i-c-h-a-l-s. It sounds like M-i-c-h-a-E-l-s, but it's spelled…"

"I get the picture, Kevin Michals without the 'e'. I'm Kara Peters with two 'es'," she said blandly, retrieving the planter and pulling a bench over to the appropriate spot, then proceeded to stand on it.

"Wait!" He called to her, jumping up to come to her side. "Let me do that. You might fall. I don't want to be responsible..."

"I can do it." Good grief! He must be used to women who can't do anything. She had to laugh to herself. If he had been one of her brothers, they would have *made* her do it herself—but then he wasn't one of her brothers. Her thoughts suddenly turned pensive. No. He *wasn't* one of her brothers. Her attraction to him was very unbrotherly, in fact. "Sure, here go ahead. I might fall and hurt myself." She tried to sound a little helpless while inside she was chastising herself for having those 'unbrotherly' thoughts about him.

"Where did you learn about lawnmowers?" he asked conversationally as he stepped up on the bench.

"You might...of course, this is just a suggestion mind you...but you might want to take an ice pick and make a starter hole for the screw. It's kind of difficult to get started in that hard wood."

"Who's doing this?"

She shrugged and sat down.

"You didn't answer my question."

She took a deep breath. "Lawnmowers? I learned to work on all kinds of motors back in Joliet at my brother's service station."

"You worked at a service station?"

"Listen, I was an excellent mechanic..."

"Okay, okay, I believe you." He grunted as he tried unsuccessfully to start the screw in the hard wood. "Joliet. Is that where you're from?"

"No, actually I'm from here—Peoria. I moved back when Barb called and practically begged me to come." She laughed. "She said she couldn't get married and go honeymooning until I got here. I'm a sucker for a romantic sob story." Her breath quickened when she realized he was grinning down at her, his eyes casting their appraisal over every inch of her body. "Well, actually, I wanted to move back. We all moved to Joliet when Mom's sister Edith became too ill to take care of herself. Mom moved me and my brother Paul there and the rest of my brothers soon followed with their families."

"The rest?"

"Yes. There are five of us kids. I'm the youngest. I have

four older brothers. Dad died several years before we moved."
She watched him struggling with the screw for a few more
seconds. "Okay, get down. I've let you be manly and rescue a
damsel in distress long enough. You're making me nervous."

"You're out of luck. This absolutely cannot be screwed into
that hard wood."

She ran to the shed and came back with a hammer, climbed
on the stool, pounded the screw into the wood part way, then
screwed it the rest of the way. She forced herself not to look at
him as she gathered up the planter and hooked the ring onto the
hook.

"Guess that about does it," she said brightly. "Now all Barb
needs is a nice plant for it."

"You do that for a living?"

"No." She laughed. "It's just one of my hobbies. I just
finished making fifteen of these for my church's bazaar to help
raise funds for the new youth center. When you're low on funds,
handmade things are the next best thing to help out." She
glanced his way. "You don't seem like someone who suffers
from lack of funds."

"No, suffering is not in my game plan," he said jokingly.

She laughed out loud. "With me it's a way of life."

He looked serious. "You mean your family was poor?"

"We weren't poor. Granted we had very little extra money,
but we got along okay." She watched his gaze grow distant. "We
had each other and our faith in God helped. God never failed to
give us what we needed. Not always what we wanted, but what
we needed."

He turned his eyes back to her. "You said your dad died
young." His voice was low. "It's nice you had others." He
studied her face for a moment then let out a nervous laugh,
rubbing his hand across the back of his neck. "How'd we ever
get on such a morbid subject?"

"It's okay. Of course, you miss your loved ones but we
know they are in a better place. Mine are anyway. They were
believers." His pensive stare troubled her. "Have you lost loved
ones?"

"Yeah. Let's change the subject. What did you say you did
for a living?"

I'm sorry. I guess I didn't make myself clear about my reason for moving back to Peoria. I took the vacancy at the Department of Children and Family Services. I work with Barb. She's my supervisor."

He leaned forward. "You do? How come I've never seen you?"

"You have…at the wedding."

"No, I mean in court. I'm a public defender. I come in contact with people from your office all the time."

"Oh no! You're a public defender?"

"You make that sound like trouble in River City."

"A lot of times it is."

"Why, because your case workers are trying to take a child out of the home and I'm defending the parent?"

She shook her head yes. "I personally would never take a child away from a parent if there was any other way."

"Then we're on the same page."

CHAPTER FIVE

She blinked a couple of times while recalling the girls in the office being gaga over the 'hunky public defender'. Of course, it had to be Kevin Michals. The girls were doing everything in their power to get a date, and according to the gossip, he'd made more than a few dreams come true.

"So, you're *the* Kevin Michals!"

"I believe I already knew that. In fact, I told you."

"No, I mean *the* public defender all the…" She stopped. She didn't want to tell him about the other girls' opinions. "Never mind." She must sound brain dead. She needed food. "I guess I'd better be going now," she told him, adding politely, "Nice seeing you again."

"Don't go. I like you Kara Peters with two 'es'. I like your sense of humor. You're a lot of fun."

"Oh, yeah, I'm a barrel of monkeys, but I gotta go."

"Wouldn't you like to stay for dinner?"

Even though she knew he heard her stomach growl, she shook her head no. She could just explain how she preferred Coney dogs over T-Bones, or perhaps she could convince him she was stuffed to the gills with caviar left over from the party she gave last night for an important dignitary, but as usual the truth came out. "I can see you're expecting company with the table set for two, wine chilling, candles…" She tapped her forehead. "I'm no fool. I can recognize a romantic date when I see one."

He laughed again at her humorous tone. "What an eye you have for the obvious, but I'd like you to stay."

"No, thanks. I wouldn't want to intrude on the 'someone else' you're expecting."

He smiled.

"Your brother perhaps? Tee hee." She smiled back, raising her eyebrow.

"Very funny. I don't have a brother."

"Want one of mine. They *love* steak."

"Probably not my type," he returned playfully sarcastic. "I WAS expecting a... 'someone else'," he mimicked, "but not now."

"Oh, poor baby. Stood up?"

"Something like that. She called while you were tending the field on the tractor." He laughed again, then seriously said, "Her mother had to have an emergency appendectomy. That kind of ruined our plans."

"Oh, how inconsiderate. I hope it wasn't intentional on her mother's part. She may have heard about your reputation with the females and was protecting her daughter."

"And how do you know about my 'reputation'? You didn't even know who I was until this evening."

They both laughed.

Kara tapped her forehead again. "I told you I was smart. I can tell."

"You're nice company, Kara Peters. Please stay. I have to cook the steaks, they're thawed. Please?" His voice was soft and appealing. It seduced her senses to the point she felt embarrassed.

She dropped her gaze from his and shrugged. "I guess it would be better than my leftover goulash or the mystery meal in the orange bowl."

He chuckled. "Mystery meal? Sounds like road kill."

"Close." Wild horses couldn't drag her away now even though she knew she should leave. She was feeling a strong attraction and that could be folly on her part. Even if she weren't suffering from the heart disorder, the chance he would be attracted to her would be highly unlikely—also, unprofessional, unethical and all the other 'uns' she knew so well. She did not want to be involved in any way with a public defender! And even with all that aside, she thought with amusement, could Kara Peters find happiness with a man who ironed his bathing suit?

"So you're staying?"

She pouted her lips. "I guess I'd be better than nothing."

"Oh, I'd put you a little higher than zero." He chuckled. "On a scale of one to ten, I'd say…"

"Don't give me your answer right now. At least give me the chance to wash the green off my feet!"

"I don't know," he said skeptically, looking her up and down, "that might lose you points. Green feet was one of your attractions." His eyes again scanned her from head to toe. "That and a few other assets I could mention."

"You're a flirt, Kevin Michals, without the 'e', but that won't keep me from eating your steak."

"Good! The coals are just about right. I'll put the meat on and you make the salad…after you wash up." He grinned.

"I promise not to make it with my feet if that's what you're worried about. Besides," she added lightly, "I thought I was a guest. Were you going to make your 'someone else' fix salad?"

"I had other things in mind for her," he said, his voice intentionally dripping with sexy innuendos.

Gulp! Why did she even ask such a stupid question? "I'll just bet you did."

"Now, if you would rather skip making salad and really fill in for my date."

"I'll make salad!"

"That's what I thought."

He was still laughing at her while she rinsed off the lettuce and vegetables.

Kevin placed the two big steaks on the grill, then came back into the kitchen to help her chop the salad makings.

She felt herself having a good time working alongside him. "I've told you about me, what about you? Small, medium or large family."

"I'm an only child," he answered quietly. "I was raised by my grandparents after my parents died. Now my grandparents are dead also."

"I'm so sorry. My grandfather died recently."

"Well, don't be sorry for me. I'm used to being on my own."

Somehow Kara didn't think he sounded all that convincing. "You never longed for…family?"

"Not anymore…" His voice trailed off and stopped short as if something had slipped out that he did not wish to divulge about himself. He laughed nervously. "When I see friends with a bunch of noisy kids and their house looking like a giant egg beater had gone through it, I'm thankful I live alone. Free. No fuss, no muss."

Kara winced. A giant egg beater? What would he think went through her house? A motor boat?

"That's another reason I'm staying here until my apartment is completely done. I hate clutter, the smell of paint and, well, I guess I'm too much of a perfectionist."

"Good grief! You must think I'm a total wreck!" She looked down at her crooked cut-offs.

"Nooo, I think you're a total…," he chuckled loudly, adding, "…cute person."

"A total cute person," she repeated blandly. "How much above a zero is that?"

"Ummm…about a four and a half," he teased.

She slung a piece of lettuce at him. "Creep!"

He casually picked the piece of vegetable out of his hair and tossed it in the sink. "You are so much fun…for a mechanic."

****

The dinner was divine. Kevin catered to her, exhibiting all the graceful etiquette she could ever imagine. It couldn't have been more elegant if she had been dressed in a silk, pearl-studded gown and dining with the Queen of England. Tonight she was a princess, dining with a prince. She prayed silently to God. *I know I'm being selfish and extremely foolish, but I'm having such a lovely time. Please grant me one evening with this delightful man. I know it cannot go any further.*

Her thoughts were interrupted with, "Would you like some wine? We could drink it out on the patio," Kevin suggested, reaching for the bottle. "Who knows…maybe the stars, the moon…a little wine…?"

"Maybe I'd better go home," she stated bluntly.

"Only teasing…sort of." He motioned for her to go ahead of him. "We can just sit out there and talk. What's your hurry anyway? Got a late 'someone else'?"

"Ha!"

"Ha? May I take that as a negative reply?"

"Not only no, but double no. I don't have a 'significant other'. I can't…don't…" Why did she blurt that out? Why couldn't she have said, not tonight? I've been out dancing six nights in a row 'til dawn and I needed the rest. God just wouldn't let her say those silly lies she thought up.

"Hard to believe a beautiful girl like you wouldn't have a boyfriend," he said seriously, taking hold of her hand.

She was openly embarrassed. She felt like a shy school girl as she toyed with a raveling on the leg of her cut-offs. She pulled her hand from his and sat down in one of the lawn chairs on the patio. Kevin pulled his chair next to hers and his presence suddenly seemed so virile, so bracing.

"It…it's been a very enjoyable evening, Kevin. Thanks for din—"

Her words were cut off with the feel of his hand on her hand again. Her eyes refused to look up. Her lids were glued shut.

"Kara?" He crooked his finger under her chin. "Look at me, Kara."

Her eyes fluttered open and she saw his focused ardently on her lips. "Are…are you going to kiss me or something?"

"Would you mind?"

"I…I think I would probably enjoy it, but…" She hadn't meant to be so honest. What was wrong with her? Her heart was pounding wickedly against the wall of her chest. It was hard to breathe. "It…it's not a good idea."

"Why? It's just a kiss."

Not wanting to go into details why she could not, would not get involved, she said, "I haven't kissed a man in a long time."

"You kissed me at the wedding."

"That doesn't count. That was an accident." She giggled to break the tension. "I mean *really* kissed a man I knew I was kissing. My pucker may be broken."

His face descended slowly and like at the movies, the screen went black. She was being tossed through the air, spinning wildly, while cymbals clanged, horns blew, and a thousand drums beat to the rhythm of her pulse.

Kevin raised his lips from hers for a mere second, a look of both surprise and pleasure played across his features. "Never in my wildest imagination would I have ever believed a green-footed auto mechanic could kiss with such sweetness." His lips began to capture hers again but she pulled back. His hand snaked around her neck with gentle persuasion and pulled her to his chest. She could hardly believe this was happening. She had dreamed it, had fantasized it and knew it could never be a part of her life, but now it was actually happening.

She pushed away. Coming to her senses, she knew this had to stop. To cover up her nervousness, she quipped, "As enjoyable as this evening was, I really have to go. I have tons of paperwork I need to get cracking on."

"Let me put your mind at ease, Kara Peters."

"How's that?"

"Your pucker is definitely not broken."

"Thanks. That's a worry off my mind. Now maybe I'll be able to sleep nights."

"Yeah," he said seriously, letting his breath out noisily as he leaned back in his chair. "I hope you can...that'll at least be one of us."

CHAPTER SIX

Kara barely remembered running around the side of the house and jumping into the safe haven of her old Buick. Then leaning her head on the steering wheel, she drew in a deep shuddering breath. These feelings! Was she nuts! Even under 'normal' circumstances, he was not her type nor she his. The other girls in her office were always fighting to fend off all the competition to gain his attention. She was NOT going to be one of those. Actually, she said to herself, coming to her senses, she was NOT going to be anything to him.

As she raised her head, she turned the ignition key. Click. Nothing.

"Come on, Betsy, don't do this to me." She tried the ignition one more time. Click. Nothing. "Don't you understand? I've *got* to get out of here...*now!*" She pulled the gearshift into another gear and firmly back to park and tried the starter again. Nothing. She laid her head back on the seat and stared at the three-cornered tear in the ceiling's upholstery. "Your timing stinks, Betsy."

She heatedly jerked the keys out of the ignition, opened the door and got out, looking hopelessly at the front door of the house. She hated to have to face him again, but what else could she do? Call Jack? At ten o'clock? That would be her last resort.

With a resolute shrug of her shoulders, she rang the doorbell. Within seconds, Kevin was standing at the opened door, his unrumpled bathing suit still neatly creased.

"I can't leave," she blurted nervously.

"Oh?" A smile spread across his face. "I didn't know I was so irresistible."

"My car won't start."

"Oh." His smile fell into a fake pout.

"Do you have a car in the garage…and a flashlight?"

"Yes, I have my car, but you wouldn't need to go you know." He smiled again. "I'd behave. Scouts honor."

She laughed at that. "Were you actually a Boy Scout? Camping out with all those dirty bugs and stuff?"

"No, but I had a crush on a Girl Scout once. Does that count?"

"Afraid not. Now get the flashlight and back your car out. I'll get my jumper cables out of the trunk and we'll try to jump-start my car."

"Hmmm, jump-start. Reminds me of that Girl Scout. I tried to jump-start a relationship."

"Just get the flashlight. I'm not interested in your past encounters."

"I'll go you one better." He flipped a switch by the door and a large spotlight beamed out over half the neighborhood illuminating the area like high noon. "What in the world is that?" He pointed to 'old Betsy'.

"What in the *world* do you think it is? It's my car!"

"Yeah, but who owned it first? Abraham Lincoln?"

"Not funny!" She walked to the back of her car, raised the trunk lid and retrieved the jumper cables.

Kevin disappeared back into the house, emerging from the garage a few minutes later in his spotless Mini Convertible and pulled it alongside the Buick. Between the bright spotlight reflecting off the shiny waxed surface of the little car and her tears of laughter, she could barely see as she walked around the small vehicle, giving it a careful once-over.

"What's so funny?" His brows knitted and he shrugged his shoulders. "What are you looking for?"

"The windup key." She laughed harder. "It looks like something off of a merry-go-round!"

He gave her a disgusted snort and turned off the motor.

"Before you clamp all that junk on my car, let me see if I can get yours started myself."

She smiled not so nicely and bowed. "Be my guest, but I tell you it won't do any good. I know old Betsy a lot better than you do."

"Well, we'll see." He got out of his car and into hers.

She climbed into the passenger side and handed him the keys. He very ceremoniously put the key into the ignition and turned it on. The same familiar 'click' was heard, followed by dead silence. Another impatient try produced the same results. "Did this have a crank that came with it?"

She breathed out noisily. "Do you know *anything* about cars?"

"Yeah. Two things. They either start or don't start. This one doesn't start."

"I can see you're going to be a lot of help—"

"Lady," he cut in, "if you had the sense to drive a car manufactured in this century—"

"You sound like my friend, Jack Bowers. He's always running Betsy down."

"Jack Bowers? I know a Jack Bowers. He works out with John and me at the gym."

"Probably the same guy. Curly brown hair, needs a shave half the time, scrawny legs, thinks he's funny? That Jack Bowers?"

"Yeah, yeah, that's him. Nice guy."

"Okay, enough small talk about mutual acquaintances. If you'll just give me your permission to 'clamp this junk' on your car, I'll be out of your hair in a few minutes, Mr. Neat-clean-and-tidy-breath, and I'll try not to get a speck of dirt on you OR your toy car." She knew her voice was dripping with sarcasm but she didn't appreciate Betsy being ridiculed.

"Ah, so you do have a temper. I guess I deserved that. I can see your car means a lot to you." He looked at her for a second or two, running his finger along her arrogantly jutted jaw until it relaxed against his touch. "Can't talk you into staying?" His voice was barely above a whisper.

"No." She pulled her face away from his touch and summoned up every ounce of good judgment she possessed to ward off the tiny shivers dancing up and down her spine.

"I didn't think so." He sighed. "Tell me what I have to do to help get this illustrious…Betsy…going."

She instructed him on when to start his motor, adjusting the cables on the proper terminals, then got in her car and turned the ignition switch. Nothing happened. She quickly got out and motioned for him to cut his motor.

"It's not the battery so it must be the solenoid."

"I've heard of that." He very astutely unclamped the 'junk' from his car battery. "Where should I clamp these now?"

She stared at him in disbelief. "Don't ask."

He laughed at her. "Well, what is it? Can it be fixed?"

"It's a little thing that sits on top of the starter. When you turn the key, it kicks the starter in, which engages the fly wheel and turns the motor over—"

"Yeah, I know, but what is it?"

"You're impossible!"

"Yeah, I know, but—"

"Yeah, I know, but," she repeated. "It can't be fixed tonight, unless you know of an all-night auto parts store."

"Well, the sensible thing to do is call the auto club."

She dropped her shoulders and stared at him. "Look at me. Look at my car. Do we look like we belong to any kind of club?" She was nearly in tears she was so exasperated with everything. "I'm afraid old Betsy is just about on her last leg."

"You talk about this old Buick like she…it…was an old friend."

"She is in a way. We've been through a lot together. She's been in our family a long time. Gramps gave her to me. She's had a few mishaps along the way and had a couple new motors put in but lately she's been more cantankerous than usual." She chuckled. "Once she dropped her tailpipe in the middle of a stop light, and her windshield wipers quit working during a rainstorm…nothing major." She let her breath out. "I'll just call Jack and ask him to borrow his boss's tow truck."

Before Kevin could stop her she had Jack speed dialed on her cell. "Jack, I need a tow home. I'm at Barb's new house. Yes, I know how late it is."

Kevin grabbed her phone from her. "Jack? This is Kevin

Michals. I am house-sitting and Kara came over to…never mind, it's a long story. It's late. I'll take her home. You come in the morning and tow Betsy. Yeah, I know, she's got me calling it Betsy. Go back to sleep. I'll get her home. What? Hitting on her? What am I, sixteen? I don't 'hit' on women." He saw Kara's wary glance and turned his back on her. "I promise she's safe with me. See you in the morning." He turned to Kara. "Holy cow. He gets a little crazy when you wake him up out of a sound sleep."

"You lied to him."

"How's that?"

"You said you didn't hit on me. You sort of did."

"You think I'd let him know that. He was irate. What's with him?"

"Don't worry about him. He's a little protective."

"A little?"

"I'm sorry about all this. I can't just leave my car here."

"Yes, you can. We'll take care of it in the morning." He put his arm around her shoulders and guided her to his car. Just before he opened the car door for her, he turned her into the circle of his arm and wiped a stray tear from her cheek with his thumb. "Hard to imagine anything getting you down. I had you pictured as someone who was always in complete control."

"I am usually." She swiped at another tear. "It's just…I don't know. Car trouble can be so exasperating. It takes a lot out of a person. Also, I've been putting in some pretty long days…extra work on my own time. There's this one particular case I'm working on that I'm pretty uptight about. This little seven-year-old girl…Teresa Becker. She just quit talking a few months ago. I've been giving her some quality time, trying to gain her confidence." Kara began to get wrapped up in relaying the facts. "It just breaks my heart…" She felt his body tense authoritatively.

"Hey, one of the first rules in your business…my business…" He tilted her face up and looked her in the eye. "You do NOT get involved emotionally."

"Yeah, I know, but…" They both burst out laughing at their repetitious use of that phrase.

CHAPTER SEVEN

The refreshing night air breezed lightly through Kara's hair as Kevin drove toward the outskirts of town where she had directed him. When they turned off the main highway onto a country road, Kevin slowed his small car to a crawl. Not that she minded the extra time he was taking, but was curious as to why he was driving so slowly.

Again, her teasing nature got the best of her. "What happened? Did the rubber band break in this windup toy?"

"Ha, ha, ha. Not funny. At least it runs." He gave her a sideward glance and snickered. "I'm not all that familiar with this road," he explained, peering out at the dark surroundings. "Where in the heck IS your apartment anyway? I didn't know we would be crossing the time zone into a world of unknown." He turned to look at her. The dim light from the moon gave her full view of his smiling face. "Besides…most girls don't like to go fast in a convertible. Messes up their hair."

She ran her fingers through her thick curls and shook her head against the breeze. "Not me. I like the wind blowing through it. Reminds me of when I was a kid and riding in the back of Gramps' pickup truck."

He laughed. "You're something else, you know that, Kara Peters with two 'es'? Really something else…" His voice trailed unexpectedly as she watched him study her face for a few more seconds before turning his attention back to the road, then gave another quick glance back at her. "You're rather beautiful in a different sort of way."

"Is that supposed to be a compliment?"

"I guess that didn't come out right. I meant you're different from most girls I know."

"I'll bet I am. And that's a bad thing?"

"Heavens no. Just different. One thing is you're a lot more fun...not so serious."

"Life is too short to be serious all the time." She thought for a moment. "Is that your type? Serious?"

"I don't have a type actually. My supposedly date for tonight is quiet, soft spoken, serious I guess you could say, but I know a lot of different types of girls." He laughed softly. "None like you, however."

"Mmmm, still don't know if that's a compliment or not." She laid her head back on the seat and mentally counted the stars in the sky and thanked God for another day.

Kevin snapped to attention, bringing himself back to the business at hand. "Are we getting anywhere near your apartment?"

"I don't live in an apartment. I live on a farm. My Gramps' farm."

He let his breath out rather noisily. "I should have known. A homeowner!"

"Gee, sorry! You make it sound like a dirty word."

"Just another thing I don't understand about you. Why would a single girl with no money want to be straddled with a house? Mowing lawns, repairs."

"Oh, you've seen my house?" She laughed. "I'm talking 'repairs' with a capital 'R'."

"That's what I'm talking about. If you lived in a...say, modest apartment and left all that up to someone else, you'd have time for other things *and*," he emphasized, "money to buy a decent car."

"Decent? I'll have you know Betsy *is* decent. I suppose you think I should be driving around in this little toy. Well, Mister Michals, I wouldn't have this if you gave it to me."

"Hey! Don't get so riled up. Sorry I said anything against old 'Betsy'."

She settled back and crossed her arms with a jerk. "I love my car and don't like your attitude toward it one bit. I couldn't even take Pooch to the vet in this thing!"

"Okay, okay. Forget I said anything."

There were several long moments of silence as the little car crept along the bumpy road.

"That's even more disgusting," Kevin finally said, speaking more to himself.

"What?"

"A homeowner with a dog."

"Turn left at the next lane." She bit her tongue to keep from saying anything. Yes, they were definitely mismatched which was a good thing, she decided. Now maybe she could get her mind off him. She contented herself with the fact they only had about a quarter of a mile to go, then he could be rid of his 'homeowner with a dog'.

****

As they pulled into her graveled drive, the small dachshund came barking from the back yard, crossing in front of the Mini's headlights.

Kevin let out a curt laugh. "I'd hate to think I couldn't get a little dog like that in this car. Heck, you could hold him on your lap."

"That's not Pooch." She couldn't help the smug smile that crossed her lips. "That is." She pointed over his shoulder.

Kevin turned just as the huge St. Bernard's head made its appearance, reaching across Kevin's chest to give Kara a friendly greeting.

"Pooch could eat this car if he wanted to." She gave the big dog a pat on the head.

"Really? He could eat Detroit if he wanted to." Kevin swiped at the 'slime' on his arm. "What the heck is this stuff?"

"Slobbers. St. Bernards slobber. He likes you."

The scene was so ridiculous, with Kevin pushing effortlessly against the huge dog, trying to get Pooch's head out of his face, that Kara couldn't contain her giggling which shortly turned into full-fledged laughter with tears rolling down her cheeks.

"Pooch, go lie down!" she finally managed to choke out.

"It's all very funny, isn't it?"

Kara managed to get her laughing under control enough to offer, "Come on in. I'll give you a wet towel to clean yourself with." She pointed to his steering wheel. "You might want to give that a wipe too."

"Ya think?"

As she opened her door to get out, the thought hit her that her house was not exactly ready for entertaining guests, but with a shrug of her shoulders, she pulled herself from the tiny car. "Mind you, this is not the Taj Mahal."

"I'm not renting the place. I only want to get dog slobbers off me." When he opened the car door, the little dog leaped up in his lap. "Oh, for crying out loud. What's this one named?"

"I don't know."

"You don't know? Isn't he yours?"

"No, he just appeared. He's Pooch's guest for the weekend."

"This is lunacy," Kevin scoffed, putting the small dog back on the ground. "Pure lunacy!"

"First thing Monday morning, I'm going to place an ad in the paper to try to find the owner. Until then, he's our guest here."

"What are you going to call him? Hey guest?" He shook his head pitifully. "He looks like a skate board…or a scooter."

Kara laughed. "You're right. In fact, that's a good name for him. Come here, Scooter." She patted the side of her leg. The little dog scampered over to her and whined for a pat. "See there? You picked a good name. He likes it."

Kevin rolled his eyes and stepped up on the back porch. As Kara took the house key from her pocket, Kevin very gentlemanly held his hand out for it.

"I'd better do it," she said, adding, "It's kind of tricky."

He breathed out noisily and took it from her anyway and inserted it into the lock, surprising them both when it opened on the first try.

"The light switch is just inside the door to your left."

He slid his hand along the wall until he came to the switch

and flipped it on. He sucked in his breath with a gasp. "Holy moly!! Kara! Stay where you are! They still may be in here!"

"Who?"

"The burglars! Your place has been ransacked!" He rushed inside, turning in frantic circles. "You got your cell, mine's in the car. Call 911. You got a ball bat or something? I'll search the place!" He was ranting emotionally. "Oh, Kara, just look what they've done to your poor house." He moaned. "You'll never get it put back together again. It would have been better had they burned it down?"

Kara took a cautious step inside, her eyes wide with expectation. She held her breath as she scanned the interior of her kitchen. A sickening feeling spread throughout her whole body. It was just as she had left it. There had been no robbery. Oh, dear God, she silently prayed, give me one of those sophisticated remarks I so desperately need right now. She could have said in a gasping voice, 'What is this world coming to when vandals find it necessary to literally destroy a place like this...to even strip off half the wallpaper'.

But God was not one to encourage tall tales. "Nothing's missing, Kevin. I...I'm remodeling before I unpack these things. I didn't see any point in putting stuff in the cabinets, then taking it all back out when I paint. It's just that I thought I would get it all done a lot sooner. It's taking longer than I had... I'm rambling. It's a long story."

He removed the rolling pin from a chair and dejectedly sat down, staring at the debris as he looked for a place to put the wooden object he was now stuck with. He shifted the rolling pin from one hand to the other, trying to locate a good spot for it.

Kara graciously took it from him, watching his bewildered look as she stuck the rolling pin in a box beneath the table.

"It all takes time...and money."

"How long have you lived here?"

"Six months."

"You've lived like this for six months?" His voice sounded shaky.

"It's not so bad. I've had other projects to work on. This was my grandfather's farm, and he was working on turning it into a Haven for troubled kids, turning the barn into a housing and activity center. When he left this world to be with the Lord, he passed it on to me along with his trust fund to be used to finish his dream. His money goes to that, the small inheritance he left me personally goes to fixing this house up." She looked around the room. "Can't you just see the possibilities of how beautiful it's going to look after I get done with it?"

"No." He stared off into space.

She shrugged. "Well, what can I expect from an…" she lowered her voice eerily, "…apartment dweller."

A small half-grin played at his features as he rose. "Are *all* the rooms like this?" He walked to the living room and flipped on the light, his eyes quickly surveying the empty space. "There's no furniture in here. You have no living room furniture. Just pieces of…" He looked closely at the scraps of jute from her macramé projects, "…rope."

She wanted to say she was saving room for the grand piano she was having imported from Germany, but as usual she told the truth. "Jute. I macramé gifts. It's a dying art, but I still do it. It's good therapy." She took a deep breath. "Anyway, I'm trying to use my own money and save my inheritance for a rainy day. I only had money for a bed, used refrigerator and stove. Gramps donated about everything he had to charity when he got sick. Maybe next pay check, I'll—"

"If you have enough left over after buying dog food." He had no sooner gotten the words out of his mouth when Smokey walked through the back door and sprinted to his side. He stood frozen as the cat stalked around his feet and slapped his paw at one of Kevin's perfect toenails. "And cat food," he added blandly.

"Yes, I'm a dreaded homeowner with a dog *and* a cat. This is Smokey."

"I was wrong. You don't have a house…you have a zoo! I expect an exotic bird to come flying at me any moment now." He walked back to the middle of the kitchen, stepping over two cardboard boxes on the way. "Do you think you can find a wash cloth in all this?"

She opened a pantry door and grabbed a roll of paper towels and proceeded to wet several sections.

Kevin stared. "What's that on the floor? An oxygen tank?"

She slammed the pantry door. "Never mind that! Here's something to clean yourself with." She tore off a few dry sections and handed them to him along with the wet ones. "You probably should be going. It's late."

"Why are you so testy? I'm the one with all the slime on me."

"Sorry." She let her breath out slowly and relaxed, berating herself for acting so childish. *Forgive me, God. I don't know what's come over me.* She knew full well what it was. For the first time in her life she had met someone she would like an opportunity to know better and it frustrated her that she couldn't. She couldn't let herself have these kinds of feelings for anyone. Her better sense told her to leave well enough alone. Get those thoughts out of her mind, but the tingles that danced down her spine when he looked at her told her better sense to go fly a kite.

Before she lost complete sanity, she turned toward her bedroom. "Goodnight, Kevin. You can show yourself out."

CHAPTER EIGHT

After taking her shower and donning her night gown, Kara walked back to the kitchen to turn off the lights. She sucked in her breath when she saw Kevin sitting on the floor peering at the leak under the sink.

"What are you still doing here?"

"Do you have any plumber's putty? I was looking for the garbage to throw the paper towels away and saw this leak. I can fix it. It looks like that little sleeve over the connection just needs to be pushed back down in place. A little putty will do the trick."

"No," Kara countered, "it's the whole fitting. It's old. It needs to be replaced. Don't worry about it, Kevin, I'll get it fixed tomorrow." She tugged lightly on his shoulder, urging him to stand up. "Don't mess with it. You'll get dirty."

He laughed. "I think that train has left the station. A little normal dirt might be a blessing compared to pet hair and slobbers."

She shook her head. "Why are you still here where you can't stand all this 'dirt'?"

"When did you lose your sense of humor? I'm just kidding with you…sort of. Get me a pair of pliers and a hammer."

"No…really, Kevin, let it go. I'll call Jack in the morning and have him pick up everything I need as well as the part for the car before he tows Betsy home."

"Do as I say, Kara," he said more firmly.

"Look, for tonight I can just put a wad of chewing gum on it and wrap some tape around…it'll keep until tomorrow. It's not all that bad."

"Will you just get me the damn tools!?"

She threw her hands up and searched through a couple of boxes for the requested tools. Finding them, she slapped them into his hand. "Here! It's a sign of limited vocabulary, you know."

"What is?"

"Cursing."

He leaned over on his side to get in a better position for his task. "You must be a…a Sunday school teacher or something."

"As a matter of fact, I *am* a substitute teacher at church."

"Figures."

"And what does that mean?"

He clamped the pliers around the fitting, his words coming out in short grunts as he tapped lightly with the hammer to slide the sleeve down. "When I was a kid, I had a Sunday school teacher just like you." He raised his voice to a high pitch, mocking a woman, "Mustn't say bad words…mustn't do this…mustn't do that."

"Well," she smiled at his funny voice, "from some of your language, I take it you were absent a lot of Sundays. Where do you go to church now?"

"I don't."

"You should. You're welcome to visit my church. It's just about a half mile farther down the road. I think you'd love our pastor." She could tell he was deliberately ignoring her.

"This is not budging," he spit out as he shifted his body and tapped a little harder. Still no progress. With a determined set of his jaw, he reared back and gave it a very healthy whack.

"*Wait!!!*" Kara yelled, but belatedly. Water spewed out in every direction, the main stream hitting Kevin right between the eyes. He jumped up and backed into Kara nearly knocking her down as she screamed her lungs out when the cold spray hit her thin nighty.

By the time she was fully aware of just what was happening, the floor was covered with water and she scrambled on her hands and knees to retrieve a roll of paper towels. She frantically unwound several yards of toweling and jammed it into Kevin's hand.

"For heaven's sake, don't just stand there. Hold this around the pipe while I turn off the water."

He was gaping at their predicament and still standing in the main stream getting soaked to the skin. "Where's the shut off valve?" He thrust the paper towels back into Kara's hand. "You stop the spray, I'll turn the water off."

She shoved the towels back at him. "No, I'll shut the water off. It's under the house."

"UNDER the house!"

"Yes, there's a crawl space. You'd never make it. I'll do it. Now hold that pipe before we both drown."

He refused to take the towels from her. "I'll show you I can do it. This is all my fault. I'll crawl under the house and turn the water off. Just give me a flashlight and directions."

Kara squatted down and held the towels up as a shield as she told Kevin exactly where he could find the valve, then handed him the flashlight. She stretched her leg out to pull a box of bath towels over near her and grabbed a handful. She couldn't have been wetter if she were floating down the Illinois River.

For some unexplainable reason she started laughing. She could hear Kevin banging around under the house. Muffled curse words filtered up through the floorboards, and all she could do was laugh and hold the towels on the pipe with a death grip. Finally she heard a frustrated, "It's off!" She was able to let go of the pipe, but she was so weak from laughter she just stayed on the floor and patted at the puddles of water with the palm of her hand.

Pooch, Scooter and Smokey were lined up in the far corner of the kitchen, staring at her with frightened expressions. Finally, Pooch sauntered over and began lapping up the water.

"Thanks, old buddy." She gave her pet a friendly scratch. "You're the best help I've had through this whole mess." Smokey and Scooter followed suit as Kara started mopping up the flood.

She glanced up from her kneeled position as Kevin came back into the house, then immediately fell over on her side as, once again, uncontrollable laughter took command. Kevin's crispy white trunks were not only soaking wet, but were now covered with mud. His 'sculpted' knees were also globs of mud, as well as his nose, chin and everywhere else.

"It sure doesn't take much to entertain you, does it?"

"Oh, I don't know. I would say this was quite a bit," she countered, still doubled over in hilarity. "Do you always go to such great lengths to show a girl a good time?"

"Get out of my way." He pushed her with his foot and slid her through the water away from the counter. He knelt down and studied the situation again.

When it dawned on her that he was not going to give up, she crawled back to him. "Hey, really, let's call it a night. I've enjoyed about as much 'entertainment' as I can stand. Remind me to wear MY bathing suit the next time."

He looked at her soberly, scrutinizing her soaked attire. "Oh, I don't know." His tone was seductive. "I don't think you look all that bad in what you have on."

She sat back, quickly moving away. Her flesh tingled when he talked like that even in jest. It made her very aware that her night gown was clinging to her like a second skin. She pulled a towel from the box and started drying herself off.

"I guess you're glad you DID wear a bathing suit." She thought a second. "Why *were* you wearing a suit, by the way. John and Barb don't have a pool."

His blue eyes raked over her wet form, lingering lazily in the area her towel was wiping. "No, but they have a marvelous hot tub. Remember?"

The towel stopped in midair as she pictured him in the huge tub with his date. She certainly never thought she would be wishing anyone ill health, but she found herself wishing it was his date with appendicitis instead of the mother. She quickly gave herself a mental slap.

"And besides," he added cockily in a teasing tone, "I look good in a bathing suit."

She threw the towel and hit him across his face. "Give me a break!"

"I'll give you a break...right in the neck." He laughed and made a swift lunge toward her. He caught her off guard and effortlessly overtook her, wiping his muddy face all over hers.

Even with all her screams and giggles, pushing and kicking, he kept her pinned beneath him.

"You're making me filthy!"

"Serves you right," he returned, their gazes locking.

She swallowed nervously. "Get up, Kevin. You're smashing me."

"Do you really want me to?" His mouth was so close to hers she could feel the vibration from his words. His lips parted in a smile and she could see the even whiteness of his teeth peeking between them. "You have a muddy face." His warm fresh breath fanned sweetly over her mouth.

"So do you." Her own lips tingled. She was aware of the weight of his body against hers and the precarious position they were in. Her arms pinned over her head made the situation even more vulnerable. A breathless moan was heard, but she didn't know if it came from her or him. It didn't matter. His lips were on hers, his tongue warmly searching for entry to the moist pleasure.

She turned her head to the side. "What are you doing?"

"I'm kissing you," he whispered against her neck. "And I'm talking kissing with a capital 'K'." His lips kissed a path to the hollow beneath her ear and breathed tiny nibbles on her soft skin.

What had started out as a teasing game was ending up something quite different. "We have to stop."

His body went limp with disappointment just before he pushed off of her. "Another accidental kiss?"

"No, I'm fully aware of who I'm kissing, but I don't want this to go any farther." She looked at her pets staring first at her then at Kevin. "A lot of good you are just sitting there with dumb looks on your faces."

"It's hard to kiss you and not think about..."

She shook her head very slowly, her eyes never leaving his. "I don't have a place in my life for this."

He raked his fingers through his hair, his voice a little stiff. "Don't you ever let down your hair...ever have a desire to..."

"I *am* human."

"But you fight it damn hard."

"Darn hard, but I wouldn't consider 'fight it' as the appropriate expression. I know you probably can have a different date every night and kissing is just part of it. I'm not, under any circumstances, like that. I'd probably fall in love or something and that is just not in the cards for me."

"You're not into men?"

"I'm not into any kind of relationship. My life is planned out and it does not include this kind of thing."

"Love? Love is over rated."

"What?"

"Nothing."

"No, what do you mean, love is over rated. Love is everything."

"I don't hold much stock in it."

"You mean you've never been in love?"

"I didn't say that." He paused a long moment, then answered quietly. "Yes, I've loved before."

She reached out and took his hand, giving it a friendly squeeze. He turned back to her, displaying a haunting hurt. "Being in love may be all right for some, but I don't need it."

Her heart poured out to him, her eyes misting. "Maybe you need it more than you think."

"Get serious."

"I am."

He let out a short laugh. "My 'serious' is short lived. I'm not the commitment type."

She laughed with him. "You don't have to tell me that. It's written all over you. For instance, you could never have a meaningful relationship with someone like me."

"What makes you say that?"

"Well, you're an extreme neatnik, I'm not. You abhor dirt, I live with it. You're a condo type, I'm not. Pets get on your nerves, I love them. You like a lot of your type women. You drive only expensive cars. One of your tailor-made suits probably costs more than my month's salary. But on the bright side, you are teeth-shatteringly handsome." She gave him a toothy grin.

"Handsome, huh? Yeah, let's go with that. Those other things probably wouldn't look good on my profile for online dating."

That made her laugh out loud. "You? Online dating? That's

46

a hoot."

"You forgot to add, I don't like messes. I've got to get your pipe fixed and then get out of here." He scooted back to the underneath part of the sink.

"Forget that. I'll take care of it tomorrow."

"But you don't have water. You can't live without water."

"I'll manage. I have a big jug of drinking water in the refrigerator. Enough for me and the pets to drink. That's all I need. I've already taken a shower."

"I wouldn't feel right. Something might go wrong that you couldn't get it fixed tomorrow...no, I couldn't leave someone in the lurch like this over something that was my fault. I'll fix it temporarily...somehow." He thought for a moment. "Do you have any contact cement?"

"Yes, but..."

"Get it."

She rummaged through a few soggy sacks until she found the tube of glue.

"This is good," he said optimistically, reading the label. "This is the kind they used to show on TV that lifts a car."

"You don't really believe all you see on TV, do you?"

She sat down in the kitchen chair and watched him smear a liberal amount on the connection after he wiped it as dry as possible.

"There," he pointed out. "We'll just wait a few minutes for it to dry real good, then I'll crawl back under the house and turn your water back on." He re-read the directions on the tube and smiled broadly. "This stuff will last 'til doomsday. You may not even need to get a new fitting after all.

Kara cocked an eyebrow. "I hope you're right." She rose and let the pets outside.

They waited patiently until the designated drying time was up, then Kevin crawled under the house again and turned the water back on. Kara squatted before the pipe, watching closely for any seepage. Kevin entered the kitchen just in time for them both to witness 'doomsday' together.

"Get the towels! I'll shut the valve back off!" Kevin's voice rang out loud and clear as water once again spewed like Old Faithful.

CHAPTER NINE

"Anyone home?" Kevin called out from Kara's porch early the next morning, juggling two sacks while trying unsuccessfully to make his way through two dogs and a cat who were treating him like their long lost friend.

Kara stuck the paint brush back into the paint can and smiled to herself when she heard Kevin's muffled demands. "Sit! Lay down! Gimme that sack!"

"Ahhh," she teased, opening the screen door. "I see my welcoming committee is doing their job. Good boys."

Kevin brushed at the tuft of St. Bernard hair that had latched itself onto his royal blue polo shirt. "Well, would you be so kind as to ask your 'committee' to take their seats…and please tell me this is NOT dog slobbers." He pointed to the damp spot on his khaki Bermuda shorts.

Kara snapped her fingers and pointed to the corner of the porch. All pets immediately retreated to the designated spot and sat obediently.

Kevin shook his head slowly. "You're amazing. How do you do that?"

Kara fluttered her fingers mysteriously and, with a gypsy accent, told him, "Magic, my friend. You know, the hand is quicker than the eye and all that rot."

He smiled at her antics and eyed her appreciatively for a long moment and his expression became serious.

She frowned. "Are you okay?"

He seemed to snap back to reality. "I'm fine. I was just noticing you are painting yourself yellow."

She suddenly was aware of her paint stained white shorts and faded tank top. Perspiration had stuck her curls to her forehead and she made a quick swipe to brush them back.

"I *am* a mess. I'm painting my kitchen cabinets…but," she raised a finger to emphasize her point, "you're wrong about the color. It is not a mere yellow. That would be much too, too ordinary for my taste." She tossed her head back regally. "It happens to be 'Canary Dust'."

They both laughed as Kevin handed Kara one of the sacks. "I bear gifts. This is for you. Plumbing fixtures."

"Oh." She pretended disappointment. "Aunt Edith always told me to hold out for jewelry from a man. Then if the affair fizzled, I'd have something to pawn…but fixtures are nice, too."

He laughed again. "Your Aunt Edith sounds like she's been around some."

"Oh, the tales I could tell." She looked in the sack again. "You didn't need to do this. I called Jack this morning and told him what I needed."

Kevin's expression grew serious again. "I also talked to Jack for a long time this morning. I let him off the hook. My mechanic towed your car to his shop. He'll be dropping it by later."

The thought of a mechanic's bill stuck in her throat like a hard lump. "I could have fixed it myself."

"Yeah, I know but…" They both smiled at that statement. "I wanted to take care of it for you. After all, it's my fault you had to do without water all night and the dryer catching on fire."

"That wasn't your fault. It was old. It came with the house."

"I'm the one who overloaded it with all those wet towels."

"I'll admit having a fire with no water to put it out with can get a little hairy." She started giggling. "I hate that your bathing trunks melted down to a wad."

"Yeah, throwing them in with all those towels was a colossal mistake."

By now Kara was laughing out loud. "I'm picturing you frantically beating the fire out with that wet throw rug while wearing my pink robe."

"Well, if you think that was funny, you should have seen the look on the neighbor's face when I had to wake him in the middle of the night...in that pink robe...asking for the spare key to John and Barb's house. He looked at me like, 'Where did that butt-ugly woman come from'?"

"Locked yourself out?"

"You don't sound surprised."

"The way things have gone since we met, nothing could come as a surprise."

He nodded. "I feel like I spent a week here last night."

"Oh, it wasn't all bad. Most of it was sort of fun."

"Ha! Fun. Last night fun?" He stared at her in disbelief. "To you, I guess having a root canal is downright festive."

"You need to loosen up a little...you'll live longer."

"Loosen up. Is that how you do it?"

"Do what?"

He cleared his throat. "Nothing. Never mind."

"By the way, what was wrong with Betsy?"

"Oh, just a little something called a solenoid." He grinned.

She smiled back. "I guess since you're paying the bill, saying 'I told you so' would be a little tacky."

"A little." He held up the other sack. "I also brought coffee and donuts...even a couple donut holes for the pets."

"Yea! No wonder they were so happy to see you. They smelled donuts!" She gave him a wary look. "Why are you being so nice?"

"Your cabinets look nice. Wow, what a difference a little paint makes to these old things."

"I told you this place had possibilities...but you're changing the subject."

He put the sack of coffee and donuts on the table and walked toward her. He put his hands on her shoulders.

She leaned back. "What are you doing?"

She literally heard him swallow noisily. "I need to..."

"Kevin, you're worrying me. What's wrong?"

He shook his head and dropped his hold on her. "Nothing. I'm just...do you know you have yellow paint on the end of your nose."

"Canary Dust." She picked up the coffee sack. "Let's have our treats on the porch."

Kevin followed her and seated himself on a rusty metal arm chair and watched the pets anxiously coming to her side as she pulled out three donut holes.

"Pray first," she said softly. Pooch and Smokey immediately bowed their heads. Scooter sat and looked at one then the other. "Head down," Kara demanded of Scooter. He laid down. "Close enough." She then looked at Kevin. "You, too. Bow your head."

He did as he was told but kept one eye on what was going on with the pets as Kara began to say Grace. "Dear God, we'd like to take a moment not to ask for anything but to thank You for all we have and to bless this food Kevin so graciously brought us. We ask this in the name of our precious Savior Jesus Christ. Amen."

She looked up and held her hand out to the pets. "Okay." They gobbled up their treats in a matter of seconds.

"Now our turn." She handed Kevin a donut on a napkin and a cup of coffee."

"You are definitely something else, Kara Peters."

"Yeah, you've told me that before."

"I mean it." He waved his hands toward the pets. "How do you get them to do that?"

"They learned fast."

"Also, I've never seen dogs and cats get along so well."

She smiled. "Humans could take a few lessons from them. No matter how different we all are, we should love one another. There's no reason for hard feelings, or war even. Love conquers all."

He took a sip of coffee and looked out across the sky, then back to her. "I've never known anyone like you, Kara."

His voice was soft and mesmerizing and she sensed something was bothering him. "Why are you staring at me again? Something's wrong. Tell me."

He put his arm around her shoulders and pulled her to him and kissed the top of her head.

"Woah! You're not going to try to start a kiss-fest again. Kevin," she cautioned. "We had that talk last night…"

"No." He reluctantly released her. "I owe you a big apology. I could have killed you last night."

"Ha! Not if I killed you first."

"No, I mean literally." He rubbed his hands over his face. "I told you I had a long talk with Jack this morning."

"He told you?"

"Yes. I had no idea, Kara. I would never have rough-housed with you if I had known about your..."

"Stop right there. I told you I lived with four older brothers. Do you think they cut me any slack just because I had heart trouble? Sure, they looked out for me, but when I was feeling okay I was treated just like any pesky little sister would be treated."

He ran his finger down her cheek. "But according to Jack, you're not just some pesky little sister."

"Jack hovers over me at times. He's my brother Paul's very best friend and has vowed to look after me since my brothers don't live here. He takes that vow too seriously." She stared down at her bare feet and wiggled her toes.

"But isn't all this work you're doing too much for you? I understand your wanting to carry out your grandfather's wishes, but—"

"Can we eat our donut in peace and change the subject?"

****

A short time later Kevin followed Kara into her kitchen and looked around the room. "I have a feeling if you had a million dollars, you'd still be driving your old car and painting old houses." He absent-mindedly gave the paint a stir. "For instance, if you lived in a small apartment, maybe you'd be able to save up enough money for some creature comforts. You deserve that, Kara. Maybe a new car?"

"Betsy is just fine!"

"Sorreee! Forget I said that." He breathed in. "I seem to be saying all the wrong things. I'm just here to help you today."

"It's okay. I'll talk to you more about all the 'creature comforts' *after* I make my first million."

"Okay, you get started under the sink and I'll finish this last cabinet for you."

"But I thought you 'detested' the smell of paint."

"I do, but since I'm already smelling it, I might as well give you a hand."

"Okay, if you insist." She laid down on the floor and skidded on her back into the under cabinet.

Later, with the plumbing fixture put in place, Kevin stepped back to admire his paint job.

"All done. If I do say so myself, I did a beautiful job."

"Brag much?" She rubbed the kinks out of her back. "I think I did all the hard work, but your painting does look nice."

"Awww, only nice? Admit it...it's fantastic," he exaggerated, spreading his arms wide to display his work.

Before she could catch him, his arm hit the bucket of paint on the counter top and, as straight as an arrow, it dumped directly on top of his snow-white sneaker. What his shoe and crew sock didn't soak up ran across the linoleum.

Kevin stood motionless, staring at his foot with a sickening look on his face. "I don't believe this is happening."

Kara had kept her mouth covered as long as she could, but the laughter was spilling out and, finally, she gave up and hee-hawed.

"Serves me right for acting like a fool. Really, Kara, I apologize. I'll pay for any damages."

"Don't worry about it. I plan to replace this old linoleum with tile."

"I know this is hard to believe, but I'm *not* usually this clumsy."

"You're right. It IS hard to believe."

"I'm just thankful I'm not this inept in the court room or I'd never win a case."

"Ohhhh, I wish you hadn't mentioned court room. I have my first court date Tuesday. A case of child neglect. I'm a little nervous."

"Tuesday? I'm in court Tuesday. What judge?"

"Let's see...Mathews, I think."

"Well, well, well." He smiled at her while trying to squeeze paint out of his shoelaces with a paper towel. "See you in court, as they say."

NORMA EATON

She leaned back. "You don't mean it. Are you defending the stepfather?"

He nodded and flashed her a very confident look.

That ruffled her feathers and caused her to rise slowly and give him a half-lidded glare. "I think maybe you'd better brush up on the 'Minimum Parenting Standards', especially the part about a parent or other person responsible for the child's welfare must see that the child is fed, clothed appropriately for the weather conditions, provided with adequate shelter, protected from severe physical, mental and emotional harm *and* provided with necessary medical care and education required by law."

"Whew, the lady knows her stuff! I'm well aware of the law, but proving that the law was broken? Now, that's a different story."

"Listen, when it comes to my kids, I'll fight to the death. Why do you think I'm finishing Gramps' dream for this Haven. It's my passion also."

"Hey, hey, hey. You're taking all this too seriously. What was it you said to me? Loosen up a little. You'll live longer. Please, I don't want to upset you. You might—"

"It *is* serious. Child abuse is not something anyone should take lightly."

"I agree, but what I'm talking about is you can't get that emotionally involved with each individual case, Kara. With your heart trouble... They aren't 'your' kids."

"Someone has to care." Her voice sounded desperate.

He took her hand and pulled her to him. "Care, yes, but you have to strike a happy medium. Care, but don't become obsessed to the point it affects your health."

She leaned against his tall, protective frame and felt soothed by the closeness. "If I had my way, I'd take all those poor unfortunate children and give them all the love they deserve. I pray that God gives me time to open the Haven and give them a chance in life."

Kevin cradled her against him. "I know you would, sweetheart. You're just too compassionate for your own good and much too sweet...oh, much, much too sweet."

"Stop." She pulled away, leaned against the table and crossed her legs in a satisfied stance. "I don't think I should be 'consorting' with the enemy about any of my cases."

His eyes ran the length of her body. She felt that familiar prickling sensation as she watched him watch her.

Suddenly she straightened and smiled nervously. "There's Coke in the refrigerator."

"I really need to go."

"I didn't mean you were an enemy literally."

"I know. I just need to get out of here."

"I could fix us some lunch. I feel I owe you that much."

He let out a long, audible breath. "I really need to go." His tone was apologetic as he nervously jammed his hands into his pockets and fiddled with his keys. "I keep feeling I'm going to say or do something that hurts you physically. That oxygen tank lays heavily on my mind."

"You're hovering like Jack, Kevin. I know my limitations and I really do enjoy your company. You can't be all bad if Pooch likes you."

"Pooch? That's at least one in this household."

"I think Smokey likes you…you never exactly know about cats, and Scooter? He likes anyone who'll pet him. And I have to admit, with all your faults I pointed out to you, I like you."

He looked intently into her eyes. "And I like you, too."

"Then you'll stay for lunch?"

"No."

Where were all the tricks and clever conversation invented for women to use like, 'You can't go. You haven't seen my valuable art collection', or, 'Gee, just when I was about to change into my designer caftan and open the only existing bottle of rare French champagne', but instead, all she could think of was, "Don't you want to see if I stopped the leak?"

She stood motionless, holding her breath as his glance once more appraised her from head to toe and back before answering.

"Sure," he said softly, then burst into a wide smile. "You're hopeless."

As she left to go under the house, he called to her, "Should I stand back in case it blows?"

The last words heard was, "Man of little faith!"

He should have never doubted her ability. Everything worked like a charm.

"Well, you have water again and everything is back to normal." He looked around the room. "Whatever you call normal."

"Staying?"

"I can't—"

Just then they heard the rattle of a tow truck coming into the drive.

"Betsy's back!" Kara squealed as she ran out the door with Kevin behind her and the dogs and cat following. She stopped short. "What did you do to her? She looks marvelous."

The mechanic smiled. "I thought a little wash and wax job was in order."

Kevin offered his hand. "Thanks, Brad, appreciate the rush job. I'll stop by later and settle up with you."

"Anytime, Kev." Brad looked the old car over as he unhitched it from his truck, then looked at Kara. "If you ever want to sell this, let me know. I know a guy who would pay good money for it. I guess you know it's a classic. This model Roadmaster was the last one they made back in the nineties."

Kevin raised his brows to Kara, but said, "I doubt if she'll ever part with Betsy."

"Betsy?" Brad laughed and ran his hand along the car's fender. "Okay, Betsy. She must like Elvis Presley. When I started her up, the radio came on by itself and it was Elvis singing a love song. I tried to turn it off, but couldn't. It finally shut off by itself, but then turned on again. Elvis sang 'My Way' that time before it turned off. It must be stuck on that old station that plays a lot of Elvis. You might want to have that looked at."

"No, that's part of her charm. I'm used to it. I like Elvis, too." Kara smiled.

"Well, to each his own, but if you ever change your mind about selling it…her…"

"I won't, but thanks."

Kara and Kevin watched and waved as Brad pulled out of the drive and headed to town before they walked back to the house. "Ready for lunch?"

"Kara, really. For one thing I need to do something about my shoe."

"Go barefooted. Try it, you'll like it." She pulled a large

lightweight blanket from one of the boxes and handed it to him. "There's always a breeze under that big oak tree out back. Spread this under it, lie down and relax…and take your shoes and socks off. That's an order!"

"You are obviously not going to take no for an answer." She shook her head no. "We need to talk."

"About what?"

"About what Jack told you. I need to explain some things. I don't want you to be scared of me."

"I'm not scared *of* you, I'm scared *for* you."

"Don't be. Now go outside and I'll fix our lunch."

****

Kevin and the pets stretched out on the blanket under the huge oak. He sighed. "She's right, Pooch. The breeze feels good."

Kara brought out sandwiches, chips and cokes for them and doggie and cat treats for the pets and after going through the 'saying Grace' routine, they all began to eat.

Kevin was pensive again and he kept looking at Kara which made her uneasy. "Kevin, I swear if you keep staring at me like I'm about to break, I'm going to strangle Jack—"

"Don't be mad at Jack. I made him tell me. I told him I really liked you but you wouldn't have much to do with me. I asked him if you had someone special in your life."

"What all did Jack actually tell you?" She took another sip of her Coke.

"I guess everything. One thing, you don't have anyone special. That made me feel worse. I thought it must just be me you don't like, but then he told me about your heart trouble, about the fact that you weren't expected to live to see your teens, about the fact that God had given you more years than any doctor could."

"That's all true."

"About the oxygen you need occasionally, about the fact you can't or shouldn't bear children." He took her hand. "He said there is nothing else they can do for you. He said you're not even eligible for a heart transplant. Surely, in this day and age, surgery or something—"

"Been there, done that, bought the T-shirt. If I had a dollar for every stint, valve, artery replacement, bypass, you name it—anyway I'd be on my way to that million dollars you talked about."

"Aren't you scared?"

She patted him on his cheek. "We all have choices, Kevin. I could live in fear of dying or feel sorry for myself, but I'm so grateful for the years I have been given and I know God has a plan for me. I'm determined to do what He wants without whining and moaning about the lot in life I've been dealt."

"I just don't know how you deal with all of it."

She smiled. "I know God, He knows me, I love God, He loves me. It's that simple."

Emotion overtook him and he pulled her to him and held her tightly. "You are the bravest person I know." His body shook.

"Are you crying?"

"Real men don't cry." His voice was shaky.

"Jack shouldn't have told you."

"He also told me if I hurt you in any way, I was a dead man."

She chuckled and pulled away. "That's Jack for you. Now eat your lunch before I sic the dogs on you."

He laid back and looked up at the swaying branches of the oak. "It *is* rather peaceful in the country…if you like this sort of thing…which I don't."

"Liar."

CHAPTER TEN

After gathering up the remnants of their picnic, she left Kevin resting under the tree while she put everything away. She wished Jack had not told Kevin what he did. She really liked Kevin and she didn't want it to ruin the friendship she felt they could have. He was fun. She couldn't remember laughing so much in a long, long time. She loved their friendly sparring. She'd been with him two days and it felt like she'd known him for years.

Deciding to take advantage of having water again, she quickly showered, put on a pink terry romper and white leather thongs then brushed her hair vigorously to relax the curls. She even applied a touch of blush and pale pink lipstick. It wasn't every day she had THE Kevin Michals for lunch. If the girls at the office only knew… She mentally chastised herself. That was a wicked thought. She shouldn't care who Kevin spent his time with—but she did.

Picking up a package of cookies and two apples, she ran back outside to join Kevin. Laughter overtook her when she saw him lying on his side asleep with Scooter draped over his knees and his back resting against a sleeping Pooch. Smokey was curled up with his head nestled in Kevin's hair. Her giggles finally roused Kevin and his sleepy eyelids reluctantly raised half way.

"Aren't you a little crowded?" She was still trying to control her merriment.

"Wha…what the hell!" Kevin sat up like a bullet, pushing and shoving but to no avail. "Get these creatures off me, Kara."

"If you will stop swearing for a moment, I'll help you. Good grief, you'd think the world was coming to an end. They're only showing their affection for you."

"Well, you know I'm not an animal person." He gently lifted Scooter away from him but the little dog slithered right back. "Kara," he pleaded.

"Hey, guys," she called to the pets, taking pity, "go somewhere else." She snapped her fingers and pointed toward the grass. All three animals obeyed without hesitation.

Kevin's brow knitted. "How *do* you do that?"

She fluttered her fingers at him again and he caught her by the wrist and pulled her down.

"I'll show you magic fingers." He proceeded to tickle her ribs.

Kara let out a squeal that brought three eager pets to the rescue. Scooter started a clamor of barking and Pooch pounced on Kevin's back, nearly knocking the breath out of both him and Kara while Smokey stood by as referee.

"For the Jees—"

"Don't you say what I think you're about to say," Kara warned sternly, "or I won't call them off."

Kevin turned to her, their faces so close their eyes could barely focus on each other. She could feel their breaths mingle when they spoke and it made her lips tingle.

"Okay," he conceded softly. "For the gee whiz." His lips vibrated against hers. "Is that acceptable?"

She tried to breathe deeply but the force of Pooch on top of them made it extremely difficult, not to mention her heart pounding like a jackhammer against her rib cage. "Very," she whispered. "Very acceptable." With as much strength as she could muster, she called for Pooch to go lie down. She relaxed a little as the added weight left and sauntered to a grassy spot. "You can get up now," she told Kevin, drinking in the feel of his nearness.

"Make me." He smiled broadly.

Her arms instinctively circled his back and her fingers memorized every muscle and bone on the hard surface. His kiss was soft and warm and sweet and she, for a second or two, cuddled into the contours of his body.

As abruptly as he had kissed her, he rolled over and sat upright, running his fingers through his hair. "We shouldn't be doing this."

"You're right," she agreed, rising, "but I don't remember starting it, so if you want to blame someone, blame yourself."

"No, it *is* your fault."

"What did I do?"

"You can't come out here and wake a man out of a sound sleep looking all pink and perfect, smelling like something utterly delicious."

"That's probably the chocolate cookies."

"Funny, I've never had a desire to kiss a cookie before."

"Don't knock it until you've tried it." She handed him an Oreo.

While they ate, Kara studied him for a moment, wondering what his life was like...this poor little rich boy. "You know, we haven't exactly acted like strangers, but in reality that's what we are. I know nothing about you except, one, you're rich, two, you're an only child, three, you are *not* a mechanic, nor a painter, *nor* a plumber—"

"Okay, okay, that's enough. List some of my attributes, will ya?" He thought a moment. "I'm a pretty decent lawyer, I care about my clients, I like chocolate."

Kara laughed. "Chocolate? That's a point in your favor."

"I think I'm a decent kisser, don't you?"

She didn't answer.

"Anyway, I haven't had any complaints from my dates."

"Too much information." She turned her attention to the sky. "Is there anyone special in your life?"

He crooked his finger under her chin and turned her toward him. "No, but why do you want to know that?"

"I don't."

"Sounds like you do."

She felt her cheeks flush. "Oh, brother. Don't flatter yourself. I was just interested in knowing what makes you tick besides wine, women and song."

"Two out of three. I don't sing."

"Can't you be serious?"

"I just try to enjoy life and don't get too wrapped up in anything or anybody. That way you won't get hurt." He turned away, his voice just above a whisper. "At least that's how it's been up until now."

"What changed?"

"I met you."

"Me? What'd I do?"

"Nothing. Never mind me. I gotta go."

His tone of voice startled her. "But…but how can you *not* get 'wrapped up' in things you care about?"

"I just don't, that's all." He turned back to her. "Isn't that what you do? Don't get involved, then you can't be hurt."

"That's not why I won't let myself get involved in a relationship and you know it. For one thing it would not be fair to the guy and it's a little bit of selfishness on my part. If I fell in love with someone, I sure would not want to be thinking about having to say goodbye any day. But you? You could. Don't you want a family someday, someone to love?"

"Not anymore."

Kara saw that sad, distant look on his face again and wondered what terrible hurt was buried deep in his soul. She reached for him. "Kevin?"

He took her hand and rubbed the top of her fingers with his thumb. "I wish things were different for you."

"Of course, I do too, but I'm fine. Please don't worry about me. I'd like for us to be friends…and I don't want you to walk on egg shells around me. We had such a fun time before…before Jack butted in."

Kevin laughed. "Yes, I feel like I've known you forever."

"I know. I feel the same and that's why I want us to be comfortable around each other. We are bound to run into one another on occasion."

"Comfortable? It's hard to be 'comfortable' around someone so desirable. Someone I usually would pursue romantically if it was mutually agreeable, but I know you can't and I respect you too much."

"Hmmm, so you think I'm desirable?"

He laughed again. "In a funky sort of way."

"Funky desirable. That works." She thoughtfully crunched a cookie.

"That doesn't mean you don't bring out all kinds of physical urges in me."

"Would you settle for a cookie instead?"

He sat back down. "Maybe one." He took an Oreo from the package.

"I'll be honest. In my 'perfect' world I dream of growing old with the man I love and him thinking I'm just as beautiful as the day he met me, and my children would have the same last name as their father, etc., etc. Is that so fairytaleish? Isn't that every normal person's dream?"

"Can I have another cookie?"

"You're evading the question."

"For some it's perfect. For me, no."

"Oh, Kevin, surely there will be a woman who knocks you off your feet. Not me, of course. What I know about you, I'm sure you've avoided girls like me. You know, homeowner, pet owner—"

"I, frankly, don't think I've ever met a girl like you."

"And that's a bad thing?"

"Both good and bad. You're a wonderful person and I can't deny you spark something in me I don't quite understand. We are so opposite in every respect." He waved his hand around encompassing her lifestyle in the country. "I don't think I have the energy you do to cope with all this."

She laughed. "Does that mean I won't be seeing you on the farm after today?"

He looked at her a long moment. "Probably not."

She breathed in and out noisily. "So…want another cookie or would that be too intimate for the elusive Kevin Michals?"

"Maybe half."

A quiet settled over them while she twisted an Oreo apart and handed him the half with the frosting on it. "Notice how nice I am to you. I gave you the good stuff."

He threw his head back and laughed. "It's hard to know what to do with you…kiss you or kill you."

"We tried kissing and that led to trouble and 'kill' sounds so final. Let's just enjoy our cookie and call it even."

He rested back on his elbow. "And what about you, kiddo? What makes you tick?"

"My interests are probably too boring for you."

"I doubt that. I haven't found you the least bit 'boring' yet." He chuckled.

She thought a moment then pulled a long piece of grass from the ground and ran it around Kevin's lips, making him pucker. "Well, my real goal, as you know, is to open the Haven...Gramps named it Kara's Haven but I changed it to Kids Haven. There's enough money in the trust to keep it going long after I'm gone. Gramps even made arrangements with a couple of retired school teachers to work as 'house parents'. They go to my church and offered to do it free, but Gramps set aside a small wage for them." She self-consciously cleared her throat before continuing. "But some of my favorite things are sunsets, wrinkles on an old face...animals...children..." She continued to trail the blade of grass along the crease in his neck and she wanted so much to add his name to the list. "...love songs."

He opened his eyes and turned toward her. "That's what you are. A song...a crazy tune that plays over and over in my mind. It's enough to drive me nuts."

"Awww, that's nice of you to think of me as a song."

For a long moment they shared the pleasure of being close, then slowly Kevin traced a finger along the perimeter of her lips and gave up the fight. A moan escaped his throat just before he pulled her to him. "The hell with it," he growled out, "I'm going to kiss you if it kills us."

She sucked in her breath. "If I don't survive, promise you'll see that the animals get a good home."

He smiled and shook his head. "You're something else."

"Seems I've heard that a few times."

The soft pleasure of his mouth was something she could have only dreamed of and she drank in the sweetness of it. She felt his hand caress her arm with tender perfection, making her tingle with excitement.

Kevin rolled her over on her back and leaned over her. Their labored breathing made them stop for air as his lips seared a trail of kisses down her neck and back to the hollow beneath her ear before he lay limply beside her, his face buried behind his arm, blocking out the world as they savored their dark paradise.

Just as a low moan gurgled in her throat, a small boy's voice was heard.

"Hi, Kara. You sleeping?"

CHAPTER ELEVEN

Kara's eyes snapped open to see Aaron, the blond-haired, five-year-old neighbor boy, squatted next to them on the blanket, his big brown eyes smiling joyfully.

Kevin moaned, not with passion, and rolled to a sitting position. "I don't believe this. How could I ever think the country was peaceful?" He stood and started gathering up the blanket.

"No, Aaron, we were just...uh...resting. Kevin, this little darling is Aaron, my neighbor."

"Swell," he answered blandly, paying the boy no mind as he jammed the cookie package into the blanket.

"What are you doing, Kevin?" Kara was puzzled by his brashness.

"I'm leaving. I need solitude." His face flushed from irritation.

Kara was becoming a little irritated herself at his attitude. "Kevin, you're being a bit hard on the boy, aren't you? After all, he's only five. He didn't know he was interrupting anything."

"I have a friend named Kevin, too," Aaron blurted out.

"Big deal," Kevin remarked.

"Only my Kevin's not grouchy."

Kara snickered.

Kevin continued with his clean-up chores, ignoring the both

of them.

"Kevin, I don't understand your attitude."

"There's nothing to understand. I've stayed long enough. Now I'm going. It's as simple as that."

Kara turned her attention to Aaron. "Honey, why don't you go home now? You can come back some other time."

"I can't. I have to find my ball first."

Kara looked around. "Is it over here?"

"Yes." The boy shrugged his shoulders. "It bounced over the fence and just distappeared," he mispronounced. "Maybe Pooch got it."

"No, I don't think so," Kara told him just before he called the dog over. "No, Aaron!" It was too late. Pooch, Scooter and Smokey came scampering from their resting places, eager to be included in the festivities once again. Pooch knocked the blanket out of Kevin's hand and the cookies spilled out, much to Scooter's liking. Smokey swatted Kevin's bare foot.

Kara and Aaron grabbed the Oreos, pleading with Kevin. "Help us!"

Aaron jumped and yelled with delight which only excited the animals more and they began running around barking and meowing and contributing their share of confusion.

Finally, Kevin hurriedly folded the blanket over the cookies and grabbed it up. "Snap your magic fingers or something," he told Kara as he ran toward the house with his bundle, half way there stepping painfully on a large dog bone with his bare foot. "Son of a…" was heard loud and clear, causing Kara to wince with sympathy pain as she watched Kevin hobble the rest of the way.

After getting the animals calmed down and promising Aaron he could have a Popsicle, she and the boy walked slowly toward the house. When they arrived, Kevin was shaking cookie crumbs from the blanket. He barely glanced up when she and Aaron stepped up on the porch.

"Kevin, I'm sorry our picnic was such a disaster."

"Disaster? You mean World War Three?" He smiled. "It never stops." His tone was very civil now which relieved Kara a great deal. "Did you get the critters settled?"

Kara nodded.

"They looked like they were dancing." Aaron giggled.

Kevin glanced hurriedly at the boy then back to Kara. "Doesn't he know his way home?"

"I promised him a Popsicle if he stayed outside with it." She went into the kitchen and returned with the treat. "If you stay outside with this and be real quiet while I visit with my friend, later you can help me with my special project for Sunday School tomorrow."

"Oh boy," Aaron exclaimed. "What is it?"

"Things to smell this time."

"Smell?" Kevin sounded very curious.

"Yes. You see, there's a little blind girl in my class and in order to help seeing children understand what it's like to be without sight, I take different things to class to recognize by feel, taste, smell...things like that. The sighted children put on blindfolds so the contest is even. This week I'm going to pick some late summer flowers, maybe take an orange and various spices, soap...you know...smelly things."

"I see. That is so like you to think up things so *no* child would feel left out."

"I do my best. You're welcome to come help."

"Sorry." He shook his head no.

She turned to Aaron. "Now stay outside with your Popsicle. I'll talk to you later." As the boy disappeared around the corner of the house, her attention turned back to Kevin. "Can I offer you a glass of iced tea?"

"Got anything stronger?"

"Yeah, grape Kool Aid."

He smiled and tapped her lightly on the end of her nose. "I really do have to go."

"I'll walk you to your car and...thanks for everything."

"Sorry I acted like such a creep."

She hesitated a moment. "I couldn't help but notice your hostility toward Aaron. Frankly I didn't feel he deserved that."

"You're right and I apologize." He drew in his breath. "It has nothing to do with Aaron personally. It's just that..." He stopped.

Kara saw that distant look come over his face again. "Is there something you would like to talk about?"

"No."

"Well, if you ever need a friend, you're welcome to come over—"

"Yeah, right. Like you don't have enough 'causes' you're concerned with already."

"Everybody can use a friend."

"Listen, Princess, you're a great gal and if I ever do need a friend..." His gaze softened. "...you'd be a good one." He laughed again. "You know if your world WAS perfect, you would find a man who is just right for you and force him to be the happiest man in the world if it kills him. Some poor sap, that is, who doesn't mind giving up life as we know it in the civilized world."

She gave him a friendly punch in the shoulder. "You know what your problem is?"

"Yeah," he tilted her chin up with one finger, "I'm looking at it."

"Seriously." She stepped away from him.

"I am serious. This time yesterday my life was running along real smooth. Then you stepped in looking like a green-toed centerfold from Popular Mechanics and I turned into an imbecile and I feel like I've spent a week here. It doesn't even make sense."

"Well, I'm glad we met and I'm not sorry for upsetting your perfect life." She wrinkled her nose at him. "I think you probably needed a little shake up."

He laughed indulgently. "Come on, walk me to my car."

As they approached Kevin's convertible, Kara's heart nearly stopped and she was sure Kevin's did. Finally, the words, "Ohhh, noooo," escaped their lips simultaneously. Inside the now not-so-spotless car sat a very sticky little boy dedicated to the painstaking task of picking dead ants off his legs where they had stuck and died in the melted Popsicle.

Aaron looked up and smiled, his eyes the picture of innocence. "I had to get out of the grass. There were too many bugs trying to eat my Popsicle." The boy stuck a leg over the door toward Kevin. "Will you help me get these bugs off? You don't have to be scared. They're dead...whoops, there's one still wiggling. I'll get that one."

Kevin stepped back. "Get him out of there, Kara," he ground out. "Just get him out."

She lifted the boy over the side and stood him beside her. "I'll get a damp cloth and—"

"No!" Kevin held his hand up in a halt, then in a calmer voice, repeated, "No. The way things have been going around here, while you were wiping the seats, the tires would probably blow out." He stepped gingerly across the gravel to the driver's side, sucking in his breath sharply as the pointed rocks jabbed into his bare feet. "I threw my shoes in your trash."

Unintelligible words filtered the air as the car spun its way onto the main road.

After a long while of just staring at the dust, Aaron's little voice brought Kara out of her stupor. "Does Kevin want to marry you?"

From the mouths of babes, she thought humorously. "Not so I noticed."

CHAPTER TWELVE

Why she felt so rejuvenated after church Sunday, Kara would never know. She certainly had not had much sleep the night before with all the troubled questions on her mind about Kevin. Not that it was any of her business, but that didn't stop her from wondering what darkness lurked in his soul to make such sudden outbursts of hostility. Also, why was he reluctant to go to church? Didn't he know he could take any troubles he has to God who will see him through anything? She knew that first hand.

What was there about him? Just something…something inside him that crept out now and again that made her heart go out to him. She scratched her head and smiled, embarrassed at her thoughts. Of course, there WAS that 'physical' thing. A kiss had never affected her quite like his. But why was she torturing herself with it? After yesterday, she would be surprised if he ever spoke to her again.

Heaving a big sigh, she hung her dress in the closet and put on some old work clothes to get ready to use her pent-up frustration to finish what she could of the kitchen. The paint on the cabinets was good and dry so she was finally able to unpack all the sacks and boxes that had been staring back at her for six months. She was thankful she had gotten the trim painted last week so she could put up the backsplash she had purchased after she got her car back. It was nice of Kevin to have it repaired for her. 'Old Betsy' must have been grateful, too, Kara surmised. She ran like a top. Not even one tiny 'clunk' or 'clank'.

A couple hours or so later with things put away, the kitchen looked great in her estimation. The tiles for the backsplash and new curtains she bought sure messed up her budget for the week, but if she packed her lunch every day, she could make it to payday and even have a little left over to pay Jack back for some of the tows.

All her decorating reminded her of her mother. They had papered Aunt Edith's room as a surprise during one of Edith's many stays in the hospital. Aunt Edith was so pleased when she got home. Kara wished for her mother tonight. Not only for her expertise in decorating but just to have a heart to heart talk. Kara felt her mom was not only the greatest mother in the world, but her best friend. She needed to discuss her 'heart trouble' she was having and it was certainly not the 'rheumatic' kind. She knew what her mom would say. "Baby girl, you know you shouldn't get involved." Kara knew that, but tell that to her heart.

By eight o'clock that evening she was through. The curtains were pressed and hung and, except for the large yellow blotch of paint in the middle of the floor, the room was nearly perfect. Pleased with her work, she made herself a tuna salad sandwich, poured a glass of tea and sat out on the back porch step to share her supper with her pets whom she felt she had neglected all day.

"Shoot," she said out loud when a glob of tuna fell out of her sandwich and onto her foot. "Get this, Smokey." She pointed to the food and the cat quickly bowed its head. "Good boy. I guess my magic fingers are still working." She laughed and pinched off bits of bread for Scooter and Pooch who also bowed their heads before gulping down the treat. Kara petted each one of them. "I love you guys."

She finished eating and leaned back on her elbows to enjoy the stars and the moon which were so bright it made the night almost like day. "Gonna be another scorcher tomorrow, boys." One thing she always remembered from her father was how to tell weather. If the stars were plentiful and bright, it was a good guess it would be sunny the next day; and, in this case, sunny meant hot, hot, hot. Even what little rain they had gotten recently only made it steamier, but she was grateful for country living. It never seemed so hot here.

Finally rousing and stretching, she picked up her dirty plate and glass. "Better go in," she told her pets, "before I steal your bed and sleep out here tonight." The drowsy animals' bodies lay perfectly still, but their eyes watched every move their mistress made until she disappeared into the house.

Kara yawned as she finished rinsing off the dishes. She would give anything to just flop into bed, but she had put off doing her paperwork all weekend and she had to bring her case reports up to date. She first took a shower and donned her shorty gown, opened the kitchen window to let in the cool night air and settled herself comfortably at the kitchen table.

A heavy feeling engulfed her when she opened the folder on Teresa Becker. She had it memorized. "Teresa Becker, seven. Mother, Wynona Becker, twenty," she repeated, glumly making note that Wynona would have been only thirteen when Teresa was born. She read on, trying to be very clinical about the whole matter. "Father, Tom Becker, alcoholic and drug abuser...whereabouts unknown. Only living relative was Mrs. Twyla Simms, aunt to Wynona Becker. Mrs. Simms in ill health and unable to assume any responsibility."

She knew Kevin was right. She *did* have too much compassion to remain purely clinical in some of her cases...this one in particular. She remembered being stunned to learn Wynona was only twenty. She looked to be around forty years old. An anonymous phone call to the Illinois Hot Line was relayed to Barb, Kara's supervisor, who in turn assigned Kara the case. Mrs. Becker was suspected of not meeting the Minimum Parenting Standards as set forth by law.

Teachers, doctors and other professionals are mandated by law to report any abuse they may suspect, but other individuals just call in on their own accord. Kara was thankful for the concerned person who reported Teresa's neglect when Wynona was on a drinking binge. She remembered Barb telling her if after her visit there, she deemed it necessary to remove the child from the home, she should take a policeman along. She knew that but assured Barb she would be fine.

Kara smiled remembering Barb had put her arm around her shoulders and given her a friendly squeeze. Barb was such a good friend. She could use a friendly 'squeeze' right now, but Barb, like Kevin, would only reprimand her for getting too emotional. Darn it, life just wasn't fair! It was impossible to tame her heart by laws and rules.

Teresa's dark eyes haunted Kara when she thought about her. The little girl had taken to Kara just as much as Kara had taken to her and those big eyes seemed to call out for help. Teresa needed to be put in a special school and Kara was working to get State Aid for this purpose. Her teacher had reported that, even with the excessive absenteeism, Teresa seemed to keep up adequately with the rest of the children until about a month before the class was let out for the summer. Teresa just stopped talking. To anyone's knowledge, she has never spoken a word since.

"Oh, Teresa," Kara uttered out loud, "if only you could unlock the secret. What did this to you?"

She forced herself to finish her call report on the Becker case, listing the results of her last visit and making notes regarding the final arrangements for Wynona to start in a rehabilitation program for alcoholics. Kara's eyes welled with tears as her mind painfully focused on little Teresa looking so frightened, the little girl's arms wrapped tightly around her mother's leg. As was usually the case in matters such as these, mother and child were very dependent on each other.

Heat seemed to close in all of a sudden bringing her thoughts back to the present. She went to the sink, wet a paper towel with cold water and pressed it to the back of her neck. She wished she could magically wave a wand and make Teresa's hurt go away.

Magic. A weary smile crossed her lips remembering Kevin's playful antics with 'magic fingers'. She absent-mindedly fluttered her mystic fingers over her head, stopping in mid-air when at that precise moment the house phone rang. Eleven fifteen, she noted by the clock. Who would be calling? Caller I.D. showed, 'unknown'.

"Hello," she answered skeptically.

"You're going to think I'm crazy for calling in the middle of the night, but…"

"Kevin?" She looked at her fingers and wondered if they

really were magic.

"Who else would be up this time of night trying to get paint off his foot?" His tone was gruff. "I even shaved the hair off the top of my foot because it was all stuck together. Now, I look like a jerk. One foot has black hair on it, the other looks like a yellow baby's butt."

Kara started giggling.

"Oh, cute. Real cute, Kara. It looks stupid."

"Unless you go to your office barefooted, I doubt if anyone will ever see it."

"I don't live my whole life in the office. I *do* have a social life."

"Oh." She didn't really want to think about that. "I guess you *would* be the laughing stock at a hot tub party," she returned coolly, then drew a long breath. "You're lucky I answered. I don't usually answer 'unknown' callers. How did you get this number?"

"You're one of the few people who still have a house phone and you're in the phone book. Sorry about the 'unknown' part. I don't like for my number to be available to everyone I... Never mind, you wouldn't understand. You're too trusting."

"Okay, okay, I didn't ask for you to make a short story long." She let her breath out noisily. "I'll tell you what you can do. I use paint thinner, but I doubt if you can find any of that, so look on Barb's dressing table and see if she has any fingernail polish remover."

"Okay, hold on."

The phone dropped with a thud. Kara winced and held the receiver away from her ear for a moment.

"Okay, I'm back." He sounded out of breath. "I've got it. Now what?"

"Just soak the corner of a paper towel or something and dab it on your foot," she instructed, "and wipe gently."

"Yeow!" he yelled, causing Kara to pull the phone away from her ear once again. "This burns, for crying out loud."

"Gently," she repeated. "I said wipe gently. Your foot's not used to being shaved. It's probably tender."

"Now you tell me."

"Poor little baby."

She heard his soft, deep laugh. "If you were here, I'd make you eat those words...or make you do something," he added huskily.

"Is this going to be an obscene phone call?" she asked playfully.

"Maybe," he returned just as playfully.

"Then wait until I get my glass of tea so I can relax and enjoy it."

They both laughed and she felt hours of tension drain from her shoulders.

"Oh, Kevin, I'm so glad you called. I needed a friend to talk to."

"What is it, Princess? Did your roof cave in or something?"

She giggled softly. "Nothing of the sort. In fact, today was rather uneventful as far as catastrophes are concerned. You should have been here. All in all it was very productive. You won't believe my kitchen now."

"I didn't believe it before."

"Well, you need to come back sometime."

"I'm busy this year."

"Kevin! Do you mean we can't even visit each other socially...just as friends?"

"I'm just teasing. Sure, I'd love to visit your kitchen again sometime. It makes the Vietnam War seem like a skirmish."

"You may have to eat *your* words after you see it."

"Not to change the subject, but you said you needed someone to talk to. Is something bothering you?"

"Nothing new...just Teresa...the little girl I told you about. I've been working on that case tonight and it's a real dilemma to me. She just refuses to utter a word due to some psychological upset that we can't determine. It's pitiful. I feel so helpless."

"Kara, listen to me once and for all. You are not helpless. You have choices in cases like this. You know that. It's spelled out in the law."

"Laws! They're so unfeeling."

"But they're the laws. They're the best we have. Let me get this straight. Are you considering removing the child from the home?"

"If the mother doesn't respond to rehabilitation, I may have to and if I comply by the 'rules'," she emphasized, "I have to first try to find a relative to take her; second, a foster parent, and lastly place her in a group home." She knew her voice was quivering. "She only has one relative, a great aunt who is too old and too sick. A foster parent would have to be a very special person to cope with Teresa's problems, and I could never in a million years place her in a group home."

"Kara..." There was caution in his voice. "You've gotten too close, too involved. You'd better ask that someone else take over this case."

"Never. I won't let Teresa go."

"Listen to yourself. She doesn't belong to you. She's an unfortunate child who needs your help...your professional help. That's all you can give."

"What do you know? You don't even care about children, period. Have you no heart?" she snapped.

Dead silence prevailed for a long period of time, then, "Yes, Kara, I have a heart," he answered very softly and caring, "and it's been broken. And I'm trying to keep that from happening to you. Listen, kiddo," he said with a lighter tone, "I've got a few years experience on you, so believe me when I tell you, just go by the rules."

"Rules, laws, paperwork. Aargh!!" She let out her frustration, getting her self-control back. "I'm sorry I was so sharp-tongued with you, Kevin. Sometimes I think I'm not cut out for this business."

"Nothing to feel guilty about. Some people aren't," he agreed, then chuckling, "I could always ask Brad to give you a job down at his garage."

She laughed. "Now, that I could handle."

"No doubt about it, Princess. No doubt about it." After a moment's hesitation, his voice brightened. "Hey, surprise! You'll be happy to know the paint is gone. I'm clean-footed again."

"Well, hallelujah! Now, can I go to bed?"

"Yep. Me, too. You gonna be okay, babe?"

"Yeah, I'm fine."

"Okay, then, goodnight."

"Goodnight."

Just before the disconnect she heard a hurried, "See you in court!"

"Ooooo, he can be so infuriating," she muttered as she stomped off to bed.

CHAPTER THIRTEEN

Kara arrived at her office early the next morning intent on beating the scorching heat that was already threatening. Although the lavender sundress she was wearing was about the coolest outfit she had, the muggy humidity made the sleeveless white loose vest she wore over it feel like an overcoat.

She put the peanut butter sandwich and apple she had packed into her desk drawer and breathed in the cool, air-conditioned air while mulling over her agenda for the day. Her reminder calendar told her today was the day to drive Wynona Becker to the rehabilitation center...but first things first.

She called in the ad for the lost and found section regarding Scooter and asked it be run for three days. Scooter was such a nice dog; she couldn't help but think his owners would be worried sick about him.

With that out of the way, her attention was turned back to the business at hand...get Wynona to the rehab center by ten o'clock. More permanent arrangements would have to be made for Teresa, but for today Kara had solicited the help of a public health nurse to come to the home and watch after Teresa until Wynona returned.

A lump formed in Kara's throat and she swallowed hard, trying to erase the feeling that spread over her as she recalled Teresa's precious hand in hers as the little girl walked her out to her car that first day. An unexpected errant tear spilled over the brim of Kara's eye and she made a quick swipe at it with her fingers.

She pictured the look on Teresa's face when she saw old Betsy…like it was the most beautiful car she had ever seen. Kara smiled to herself. Probably because she had never seen a car that old. Teresa thought it was something new. The little girl rubbed the door panel very gently and trailed her tiny fingers over the fender, kissing the dent near the headlight to make it better.

Tears were spilling faster now just thinking about Teresa. Embarrassed by her lack of composure, she cleared the lump in her throat, grabbed a tissue and went to the ladies' room to freshen up before the other office workers noticed her tearful musings.

As she returned to her desk, the receptionist told her she had had a call from Wynona Becker saying she couldn't make it to the center today.

"Oh, yes she can!" Kara grabbed the phone and punched in numbers with the speed of lightning. "She is going to make it if I have to drag her."

"Hello," came Wynona's voice from the other end.

"This is Kara Peters. I'm on my way over to pick you up," she said very cheerful, covering up her anxiety. "Has Mrs. Traub come yet?"

"I called her. I can't…didn't you get my message? I'm just not up to it. I think I'm coming down with a cold."

This was very typical for people in Wynona's situation. Any excuse to keep from facing reality. They had such a fear of reality.

"Sure you can go. Once you're there, you'll feel a lot better. Trust me. I'll be with you," Kara promised, looking at the stack of folders on her desk that needed looking into.

"You mean you'll stay there with me?"

"Sure," Kara answered pertly like she had nothing else in the world to do.

"Well, maybe."

"Good. I'll call Mrs. Traub back and pick you up around…" She looked at her watch which had stopped again, shook her wrist vigorously. Nothing. "Soon." There definitely was a new watch on her 'when I get rich' list.

****

Kara got Wynona registered and stayed with her during the first session which seemed to go extremely well, giving Kara a more optimistic outlook for Teresa and Wynona's future. By the time she got Wynona back home, there was only time for one more call to a family who had been recently reunited. So far it appeared to be one of the few 'happy ending' cases Kara had dealt with.

She did not return to the office but went directly home to get prepared for her 'day in court'. Her nervousness was only enhanced when she thought about Kevin being pitted against her in a court battle. Surely, if he knew the facts of the case, he wouldn't have the heart to defend a stepfather who habitually left a three-year-old girl to fend for herself as he slept all day stoned on drugs while the mother worked. Kevin surely could find no defense for that down deep in his heart.

Kara's mind drifted back to their conversation when Kevin had indicated he had had his heart broken. She also thought about the times when that haunting distant look came into his eyes. Yes, there was a very private part about Kevin that he tried to keep well-hidden, and Kara wondered if she would *ever* know the hurt behind that look. God knew. She prayed Kevin would turn to Him for guidance.

After a light supper and shower, she retired early, wanting to be fresh for her court date. She went to sleep mumbling, "Juvenile Court, Peoria Court House, ten o'clock, see Kevin. Mmmm, Kevin. A smile formed easily across her sleepy face as her last thought drifted her into dreamland.

****

Ten o'clock sharp Tuesday morning, Kara, dressed in a crisp navy blue linen suit with a white eyelet camisole underneath the jacket and clicked her navy high-heeled pumps across the courthouse floor toward Juvenile Court. Just as she was about to enter, a voice called from behind.

"Morning, Ms. Peters."

She didn't have to turn around to know it was Kevin. When she did, her heart quickened and breathing could only be accomplished in shallow breaths. She didn't think it was possible for him to be any better looking than when she first saw him, but his light gray business suit, tailor made to fit like a glove, made him even more so. There was a pale blue stripe in the material that was the exact color of his eyes and his dark features contrasted nicely against the gleaming white shirt and blue tie.

She smiled a greeting. "Morning, Mr. Michals."

They both entered the court room together and as they walked up the aisle to their designated tables, Kevin leaned close to her ear and whispered, "You look mahhhhhvalous! Did you dress like that to distract me?"

She stifled a giggle, biting her lips together. "Of course. Otherwise I would have worn my bib overalls." He may not know it, she thought wickedly, but he put new meaning to looking 'mahhhhhvalous', and she knew if she was going to keep her mind strictly on business, she was going to have to keep her eyes off him.

The case was not cut and dried as Kara had hoped and, when court adjourned later that day after a short lunch break, she was disappointed it had not been settled. The Judge's, 'Court will reconvene tomorrow at ten a.m.', made her wince at the thought of another day away from the stack of reports on her desk. If it wasn't settled tomorrow it wouldn't be heard again until next Tuesday since Juvenile Court was only held on Tuesdays and Wednesdays.

She sighed wearily as she gathered up her papers and slid them into her briefcase. She was tired, but satisfied she had done a good job so far, getting in more points for her side than Kevin appeared to have done for his. She was quick to note, however, he was excellent and she hoped she never appeared in court with him if she didn't have a solid case.

She glanced up sensing someone approaching her after most others had left. "Can I carry your books?" Kevin offered. "I thought I might take a sneak peek at your notes and learn your strategy."

"Oh, no you don't. I think I have enough strength left to carry my own stuff." She added with mock politeness, "But thanks anyway."

"I'll walk you out then."

"I don't think I'm supposed to be 'consorting' with you."

His eyes gave her a sexy look. "Consorting comes later…right now it's just walking. But if you get into trouble, I know a good attorney who would be glad to handle your case."

"Ah, ah, no flirting, Mr. Michals." She wagged her finger at him. "It'll get you nowhere."

He laughed and took her arm to escort her out of the courthouse. "How about going somewhere for a drink to celebrate my victory?"

She rolled her eyes. "One, I don't drink and two, more importantly, you did not win."

"Well, then, let's celebrate a tie."

She shook her head. "I have things to do."

"I know what," he said ignoring her protests. "Summer Theatre is putting on a musical this week in the park. I've got tickets. Wanna go?"

"Don't tell me another mother's appendix burst." She laughed.

"No, nothing like that. You're not 'filling in' for anyone this time."

"Sorry, can't tonight. I put an ad in the paper trying to find Scooter's owners and it has only one more day to run. I used my land line phone number. I don't want to be away in case someone calls," she explained as they reached her car.

Kevin walked around to the driver's side with her and opened the door. "The tickets aren't for tonight."

"When are they for?"

"When do you want them to be for?"

She settled in behind the wheel and peered skeptically at him out the open window. "I thought you already had the tickets."

"I lied."

She grinned back at his teasing smile. "What was all that talk Saturday about 'avoiding me at all costs'?"

"Hey, I'm only trying to be 'friends'."

"Oh?"

"We have a lot of fun together."

"We do?" she asked playfully, thinking about all the disasters that happen when they were together. "Since this play is performed in a tent, aren't you afraid with us there it'll collapse?"

"I'll take the chance if you will. I know a girl in the play and she can get us really choice tickets."

Of course, he knows a girl in the play. "Never mind. I don't think your girlfriend would like to get tickets for you to take another girl to see her."

"Hold on. She's not my girlfriend. She's Jack's friend. I doubled dated with them a few times."

"You mean Terri Lou?"

"You know her?"

"Of course I know her and I've seen her in productions before. She's great."

"Then you'll go?"

She studied him intently for a long moment, his eyes penetrating into hers. Looking at her like he was, he was making an offer she couldn't refuse.

"Okay, how about Friday?"

"Friday's great," he said exuberantly. "I'll pick you up around six. We can have dinner first."

"This is not a date, is it?"

"Heck no...just friends enjoying a play together."

"Super," she called to him as the loud roar of Betsy's engine broke the sound barrier.

She watched him in her rearview mirror, still covering his ears and shaking his head as she turned the corner and Betsy's radio blaring a familiar Elvis tune.

"Friends, huh?" she muttered out loud. Isn't that what she wanted? Could her heart keep it 'just friends'?

CHAPTER FOURTEEN

K ara had set her alarm for three in the morning Wednesday to finish reports she had neglected to do the evening before. Aaron had come over to 'play' and she found it much more fun to frolic with him in the icy spray of the sprinkler than to sit in a hot house and sweat over paperwork.

Now she was paying the price for her wayward ways. It was fifteen minutes before court session and the back of her eyelids felt like sandpaper as she pulled into a parking place near the courthouse. Yawning, she gathered up her files and briefcase and stepped out of the car, straightening the skirt of her red cotton dress. She barely remembered dressing this morning but the white bib inset on the front of the bodice told her at least she didn't have her clothes on backwards.

Breathless, she made it to Juvenile Court with little time to spare. Kevin was already seated and raised his brows to her in silent greeting and she noted his eyes never left her until court convened. From then on the battle was on and when it was over, Kara felt emotionally drained as well as physically exhausted. She didn't exactly lose her case, but she didn't win either. The Judge ruled to leave the child with a relative temporarily since the stepfather had agreed to enter a detoxification program and counseling along with the mother. The case was to be reviewed in six months.

"Good work, Ms. Peters," Kevin said as they were leaving.

"Obviously not good enough, Mr. Michals," she returned heavily, snapping her briefcase closed.

He frowned. "What did you want? The parents locked up and the key thrown away?"

"Something like that." She was tired and testy and certainly didn't feel like discussing the outcome with the man who had convinced the Judge that the stepfather could be rehabilitated. She turned and walked out of the room at a fast pace.

"Hey, wait up. You act like I'm on trial here."

She turned her head slightly to look at him over her shoulder. "You know as well as I do that man can never stay straight for any length of time."

Kevin caught up with her and took her arm. "We don't know that. Good grief, don't you think the parents deserve a chance to prove themselves." His voice raised. "You people are always so hot to remove children from their home."

"We people!"

"Hear me out. In some cases, I'm sure it's necessary, but parents are human, too."

"Human!" She whirled on him. "You call it human to let a three-year-old wander around the neighborhood in dirty underwear asking neighbors for something to eat? Do you call it human to spend every cent on drugs instead of food? Do..." her voice wavered.

"Just hold on." He grabbed her by the shoulders. "I didn't say what the man did was right. All I'm saying is that if he is as willing as he says he is to make a home for her and her mother, I say give them every chance the law allows."

"Oh, yes, the law."

"Yes, the law. That's all we can go by." His voice lowered and became more compassionate. "You've done all you can do right now. The child is being well looked after and we'll just have to see when the six months are up."

They just didn't see eye to eye on much of anything, Kara admitted to herself, and there was no sense in arguing about it on the courthouse steps. Her shoulders sagged and she drew a long breath. "It's been a long day, Kevin. There's no point in our beating a dead horse to death. All I want to do is go home and get out of this rat race."

The corners of his mouth lifted in an understanding smile and he gave her shoulders one last friendly squeeze before letting her go. "Are you feeling okay?"

She looked up at him. "You're hovering again."

"Just making sure you're taking care of yourself. These last two days seem to have taken a toll on you. You need to avoid stress."

"Been talking to Jack again?"

"No, I googled all kinds of heart trouble...and surgeries."

"Okay, I can see I'm going to have to fill you in on everything that's been done to me. I wanted to save you all the details, but since you're not going to give it up, we'll talk. Googling heart trouble may not give you a clear picture."

"I'm all ears."

"Not tonight. I have important things to do at home."

"Like what?"

"Shave my legs."

They both laughed as they went their separate ways.

****

Washing old Betsy had always been good therapy and this time was no exception. Half way through scrubbing the whitewalls, Kara was already feeling the tension of the day subside. In fact, she was so intent on her diligence she didn't hear Kevin's Mini drive up and only until she heard, "Hi!" did she even know anyone was on the place.

"Hi, yourself." She rinsed off a wheel. "Didn't think you ever wanted to come to the farm again." She wasn't sure she was all that happy to see him.

"Peace offering." He retrieved a large pizza box from his car. "Just a small token of apology for this afternoon. There was no need to discuss the case. I hated putting stress on you."

She wet down another wheel and began scrubbing it with a steel wool pad. "You needn't apologize any more than I should and you did not put undue stress on me. Stop worrying about me. We each have our opinion. We'll probably get along just fine if we avoid talking about the case."

"I'm all for avoiding."

"So you've told me."

He grinned at her innuendo. "Let's eat this before it gets cold."

She nodded and turned off the nozzle on the hose. "You want to eat inside or outside?"

"Remembering our disastrous picnic, let's try inside this time."

"Okay, I'll fix us something cold to drink."

He followed her through the back door, turning a big circle when he reached the kitchen. "Holy Cow, where am I?" He took another long look. "You did all this by yourself?"

"Yes."

"You put this tile up?" He rubbed his hand over the smooth surface of the backsplash.

"Yes, again."

He continued walking around the room touching first the curtains, then opening cupboard doors, then inspecting the wall decorations, ending up in front of the old refrigerator. He gave it a once over. "I guess you're keeping this to match that disgusting blotch of dried paint on the floor."

She laughed. "I plan to get a new one someday, but in the meantime, it runs."

"Too bad it can't run off." He opened the door to view it inside. A sickening look came over his face. "Is that stuff in the orange bowl edible?"

"Only if you have a death wish."

He shoved the door shut with his elbow. "You really need a keeper."

"You applying for the job?"

"Afraid I couldn't handle it."

Her teasing nature took over again. "Awww, you underestimate yourself. I really think you could do nicely."

He sat down at the table and took a sip of iced tea. "You're going to get yourself in a whole lot of trouble talking like that."

"Promises, promises." She laughed and stuck a big bite of pizza in her mouth.

As a complete surprise, he leaned over and kissed her bulging mouth. "I've wanted to do that all day."

She tried to speak, but all that came out was, "Whum gom

fum."

"Don't talk with your mouth full," he scolded, kissing her once more.

She swallowed hard and emptied her mouth of food. "You don't play fair. You had me at a disadvantage."

He laughed. "I can't imagine anyone having you at a disadvantage. Here, have some more pizza." He jammed a piece against her mouth, smearing it up to her nose.

"Why you!" She threatened him with a piece twice as big.

"Kara! Remember your nice clean kitchen." He leaned back away from her.

"I'd rather try to remember your nice clean face after I'm through with it!"

Before she could carry out her massacre, they both fell into a fit of giggles they couldn't seem to control. She knew it wasn't really all that funny, but whenever one would stop laughing they would look at each other and start all over again.

"I don't know who I've ever had so much fun with, Kara." He sounded serious all of a sudden

"Yeah, like I've told you, I'm a barrel of monkeys."

The mood had changed and they ate the rest of the pizza in relative silence.

Finally, Kevin wiped his mouth with a napkin and smiled at her. "You said you were going to tell me about your heart trouble."

"Some other time, Kevin. Let's not ruin a nice evening with serious talk."

He took her hand. "No time like the present. I want to know."

"Okay. Here goes and don't be feeling sorry for me. I've lived with this all my life."

"When did it happen?"

"I was born with a serious heart defect. They didn't expect me to live, but God had other plans and with oxygen, I lived another two years. Then I had rheumatic fever. Again, not expected to live, but as you can see, I did. That damaged my heart even more. My body produced antibodies to fight the bacteria, but instead the antibodies attacked my heart and tissues around it."

"What did they do about it?"

They replaced my heart valve but with all the other damage it forces my heart to work harder to pump blood. I had to continue with the oxygen through several years in grade school, but before my freshman year in high school, they did a quadruple bypass."

"I read about bypasses on google. They take a vein out of your leg…"

"I know what they do, Kevin."

"I read about rheumatic heart disease also, Kara. It can cause the heart to fail."

"I also know all that." She patted him on the hand. "I said don't feel sorry for me."

"How can I help it? This is serious stuff."

"You think I don't know?"

"How can you be so…can't they do something?"

"It's in God's hands. I've told you that. We have to put our trust in Him."

"I wish I believed, but I don't anymore."

"Kevin. Why?"

He rubbed his face and around his neck. "Can we talk about something else?"

She knew it was not the time to pursue his non-believing, but it broke her heart. "If you need a friend…"

He admired the room once more. "You got anymore decorating to do?"

"Lots, why?"

"I thought maybe I could help you."

She let out a big, "Ha! For someone who couldn't stand this place, you have sure been spending a lot of time here."

"Just trying to be helpful."

"I plan to paint the utility room."

"Tonight? Can I help?"

"No, I'm going to go to bed early."

"Can I help you do that?" He smiled and winked at her.

"No."

"I'm teasing…sort of." He smiled again.

She was glad to see he was his old self again as she watched him gather up the empty pizza box and napkins and dump them in the trash. "Kevin, sometimes I wish I could just have a casual attitude toward sex, but even if I didn't have my problem, that isn't my nature."

"I know." He touched her cheek. "And I wouldn't want you to be any other way."

"Liar," she said softly with a smile.

"You wouldn't kill a guy for trying, would you?"

"Maybe."

They both laughed. "Guess I'll get going so you can get on with your rat killing."

"I'm washing my car."

"Time better spent rat killing." He walked her back out to 'old Betsy'. "Why bother?"

"There's a lot of us not in the best of shape, but we bathe."

"You're dreaming if you think it will help." He slapped the hood with the palm of his hand.

Betsy's horn immediately honked and stuck in a deafening mode. Kevin jumped about two feet in the air backwards. "What the…"

Kara lifted the hood and, with her magic fingers, stopped the blare. "And *you're* dreaming if you think Betsy will take your bad-mouthing." She laughed and slammed the hood closed.

"Sorry, Betsy." Kevin bowed to the Buick, then to Kara. "Excuse me if I forget your car is human."

They laughed together as Kara picked up the hose to resume her car wash.

"Speaking of dreaming," Kevin commented playfully, "I had a dream about you last night."

"Oh?" She eyed the cocky grin he had on his face. "How much do you owe me?"

He chuckled seductively. "You should pay *me*. *You* had a terrific time."

"What about you?"

"Average." He rocked his hand in a so-so manner.

A blast of ice cold water hit him squarely in the face and he gasped for breath when she directed the hose to a lower part of his body.

"You've ruined me for life! Dammit!" He sputtered as water shot into his gaping mouth.

"No cussing or I'll wash your mouth out again."

He held his hand up against the spray and wrestled the hose away from her. "Now, let's just see how brave you are."

She ran squealing across the yard as he sprayed her retreating body. Pooch, Scooter and Smokey soon intervened, barking, snarling and hissing. Their persuasive insistence became hostile and not to be reckoned with which forced Kevin to lay the hose down and put up his hands in surrender.

"Okay, okay, nice doggies, nice kitty…Kara, do something!"

Kara called to them, snapping her fingers and pointing to the porch. They immediately fled to their spot.

"I can't believe those crazy animals." He seemed a little shaken. "How come they didn't throw that fit when you were attacking me?"

"You don't hold your mouth right, as Aunt Edith would say." She laughed and put her arm around his waist in a friendly hug.

"I don't believe these last few days," he said seriously, walking with her toward his car. "Look at me. What's wrong with this picture? I'm an attorney respected by my peers, pillar of the community, dedicated to many worthwhile pursuits, yet I stand before you soaking wet from a water fight with pizza smeared from ear to ear. Now I ask you. Is this any way for a thirty-four year old man to act?"

She shrugged and smiled up at him sweetly. "Works for me."

"You know how irresistible you are to me right now?" He ran his fingers through the mat of curls on the side of her cheek and smoothed them behind her ear. "I'm not doing a very good job of avoiding you, am I?"

She tilted her face up to get a better look at him. "That was your idea, not mine."

"Kara," his voice was husky, "I don't want you to think I would ever take advantage of you, but you've got to know you bring out feelings in me…"

"I know." At least he was honest. She knew what to expect…or in this case, what not to expect. A wide grin suddenly crossed her face when she looked at his solemn expression.

"Well, are you going to kiss me goodbye or not? As friends, that is."

His grin matched hers. "Damn right." He pulled gently at her bottom lip with his teeth.

"Stop swearing," she whispered against his mouth just before he engulfed hers with mind-boggling delight.

He pulled away and muttered something about having to go. She tried to breathe normally but failed. "Wow," she barely uttered, trying to make light of the situation, "with a little more practice, you'll have that darn near perfect."

He let out a tension relieving laugh. "You are so right. You *are* a barrel of monkeys."

CHAPTER FIFTEEN

For once Kara was thankful for a trip scheduled the next day. She had to drive to Galesburg to pick up two teenaged sisters who were being placed with foster parents in Peoria. The drive gave her time to try to sort out her puzzling relationship with Kevin. She would have to be numb not to sense he had some feelings for her.

Was it more than just friends? To be honest with herself, she had feelings for him too, but she didn't want that to stand in the way of mere friendship. She had more fun with him than she had had in a long time. Sure, they were opposites. She guessed it was true...opposites attract? That was just the point. Attraction. Physical attraction.

She picked up her charges, brought them back to Peoria and happily delivered them to their anxious foster parents. The smiles on everyone's faces were worth every long hour Kara had spent finding just the right home for the twins.

Having gotten home earlier than expected, she plunged into prepping the walls in the utility room and caulking the window pane before painting the trim. With that much done, it took no time at all to paint the small room since the walls were paneled half way up. She sighed and opened the door to let the pets in.

"Hey guys, see how nice the utility room looks."

They stared at her and whined for a treat.

"Okay, okay." She handed them each a snack after they

obediently bowed their heads. "I love you guys. You're the best."

After her long cool shower and shampoo, she dried her hair, coaxing the curls to lay in a flat 'sophisticated' style. She then pampered herself with a manicure and pedicure and mentally chose the outfit she would wear on her 'date' with Kevin. She chose a turquoise halter dress with a matching belt clasped together with a huge mother-of-pearl buckle. Her shell earrings and necklace were the perfect compliment. With that settled, she slept like a baby.

****

The next morning she drove Wynona to the rehab center and made arrangements for her treatment, making sure Teresa was well looked after by a reputable lady. Kara promised Teresa she would pick her up someday soon and take her to the farm to play with the pets.

By late afternoon at home, she had paced a hundred miles and thought six o'clock would never come. She was so anxious to see how things would be between her and Kevin under 'normal' circumstances, away from animals, paint and neighbors, she was ready by five forty-five. By six-o-one, she was sure he had changed his mind and she was being stood up, but when the dogs began barking three minutes later, her heart sprang back to life.

"Hi," he greeted her at the door, giving Scooter a gentle nudge to keep him from licking his shoe. "I take it no one claimed this mutt."

"Sadly, no." She sighed. "I guess someone just dumped him. They do that a lot in the country."

He handed her a yellow rose. "For you, my lady."

"Aww, Kevin, how sweet…and I have nothing for you."

"I'd be forever indebted if you'd give me a glass of ice water. I'm parched. I don't know how you stand this heat." He ran his finger between his shirt collar and neck.

"Why don't you take your tie off," she suggested as she pried at the tray of cubes stuck in the frosted freezer compartment. "Tent theatre isn't all that formal." She grunted, unsuccessful in her attempt to retrieve the ice tray. "How would you just like to have water…no ice?"

He gave the refrigerator a long, hard stare. "You know, I could heave that monstrosity in the nearest ditch and get you a new one—"

"You most certainly won't!" She let out a huff. "Why I wouldn't even think of accepting gifts like that from a man."

"For crying out loud, if you aren't something." He took the glass of water and drank it down. "I've bought women gifts before…that cost a lot more than a refrigerator."

"And you talk about me pouring money down a sink hole."

"I never felt like it was wasted."

"No, I'll bet it wasn't, but why bring up your sex life."

He laughed at her. "That's not what I meant. I meant I enjoy buying things for people that give them pleasure." He smiled down at her. "Oh, I know. You're holding out for jewelry…something you can pawn."

"Oh, shut up."

He laughed again. "You could always pay me back out of your first million."

"Shut up twice."

As they walked to his car, he glanced toward the Kids Haven. "Looks great. Is it done?"

"Just a few minor touches in the rec room. I'm just waiting for the inspector to give me the go-ahead." She sighed. "I just hope there are no glitches. I want it to be available for use by fall."

He put his arm around her shoulders. "If you have any problems, I know a good lawyer who'd be glad to handle things for you."

She eyed him up and down. "I don't think I can afford a fancy-dressed lawyer like you."

"I promise I'll wear my cut-offs and grungy shirt."

"Ha! I can bet you don't own cut-offs let alone a grungy shirt."

"I could borrow them from Jack."

At that they both fell into a fit of giggles.

****

By the time they arrived at the restaurant in Kevin's convertible, her 'sophisticated' hairdo looked more like Little Orphan Annie's, but Kevin assured her she looked fine. In fact, he had complimented her several times on how nice she looked in that color dress. Naturally, Kara thought he was devastating in his light tan summer suit, but encouraged him to go without his jacket in this heat.

"It's going to rain," she told him as they drove around hunting a parking spot. "You'd better put the top up before we go in."

"The weather man said no rain in sight for days."

"Flies are biting...it'll rain."

He pulled into a spot and then turned toward her. "Flies are biting? Is that some more of Aunt Edith's sage advice?"

"Yes," she answered matter-of-factly, "flies bite...it rains."

"It is *not* going to rain." He turned the motor off, got out and came around to her side to open her door.

"Okay...have it your way."

Halfway through the third act, a clap of thunder shook the huge tent and the rainstorm of the year pelted against the thick canvas. It suddenly looked like Exodus with people scampering toward the exit to their vehicles. In Kevin's case, sheer panic was written all over his face as he grabbed her hand.

"Come on, let's go!" He was yelling at the top of his lungs.

"Wait." She pulled a small pouch from her purse which contained a clear plastic poncho. She very ceremoniously shook it out, draped it over her shoulders and tied the hood on her head as he stood looking irritably astonished that she was so prepared. Then in a very small voice, she said, "A fly bit me."

They hurried to the very wet convertible with Kevin sputtering instructions for her to help get the boot off since the automatic button didn't want to work and they could not get the top up. The boot finally came off, but the top wasn't about to be that charming. They even yanked and pulled by hand but to no avail.

Kevin pounded on the seat in a temper tantrum. "I cannot believe my damn luck...I just can't believe it."

Kara decided this wasn't a good time to mention his

swearing so she suggested he drive to some kind of shelter where there was light to see what they were doing. "The hinge is obviously hung up somehow, but in this downpour we're not able to see anything."

Kevin started toward the exit, and with the speed of a snail with all the other motorists, left the park in search of the nearest service station. "Whatever you say, Miss Auto Mechanic."

Kara couldn't look at him without laughing. It was raining so hard on Kevin's head that his hair parted in the middle and bangs plastered against his forehead. He looked exactly like one of the three stooges. By the time they reached the station, she was doubled over trying to stifle her giggling.

"You find the sickest things amusing." He shook his head. "My car is flooded and you're laughing."

She was half laughing and half crying. "I'm not laughing at the car," she blurted through giggles. "Look at yourself in the mirror."

He glanced up. "Who is that? I don't even recognize myself." He, too, started laughing. The station attendant looked at them like they were both crazy, but he got the top 'unstuck' and they were soon on their way.

"Sorry we didn't get to see the end of the play," Kevin apologized.

"If you had more faith in my fly story, we wouldn't be in this mess."

He gave her a wary glance. "If it wasn't this, it would have been something else. You notice how trouble follows us around? And it usually involves water."

She sat up straighter. "At least the tent didn't fall down on us."

He nodded. "We can always be thankful for that." He swiped his hair back from his forehead. "Do you mind if we stop by my apartment so I can get out of these wet clothes?"

Kara shook her head. Her poncho had kept her dry, but she noticed he didn't have a dry spot on him. "Aren't you staying at Barb and John's?"

"My apartment is finished so I moved back. The newlyweds are supposed to be home this weekend."

"I know. Barb called the office today. They had a ball. She

said she didn't want to come back, but I told her if she wasn't in the office Monday morning, I was sending the authorities after them."

Kevin laughed along with her. "I'm having my cleaning lady go over there tomorrow and spit polish the place before they get back Sunday." He turned into his parking space.

"Oh, puff, puff," she said very haughtily, pretending to smoke an imaginary cigarette, "and I'll have my chauffeur 'fetch' them from the airport."

He grinned. "I guess 'my cleaning lady' did sound a little uppity."

"A little," she agreed, admitting, "but it *is* nice of you. So, your place is finished?"

"Yep...oh, that reminds me. There's a real nice one-bedroom apartment for rent in my building that would be perfect for you, *and* you wouldn't have to worry about anyone 'dumping' animals at your door."

"No, thanks," she returned, "but that reminds ME. There's a 'dream' farm for sale about a mile from me that would be an excellent investment for you. Ten acres...a big work shop, beautiful trees—"

"Thanks, but no thanks."

She laid her head back dreamily. "If I had the money, I'd buy it in a New York minute. It would be perfect for another child care center. It's right next to the church."

"Maybe it'll still be for sale when you get your million," he teased, chucking her under the chin.

"Yeah, maybe."

CHAPTER SIXTEEN

Kara followed him through the apartment to the kitchen and put her wet poncho in the sink.

"I'm going to my room to change. Give me a couple minutes. Make yourself at home...MY home, not yours. I don't think this place needs any redoing."

She gave him a smug look. "Oh, I probably could find something."

She waited the designated time, then began to give herself a tour of his apartment. It was beautiful, but very masculine. She wandered into what was the guest bedroom and saw a huge king-size bed which looked like heaven to her. The teal green satin comforter was so fluffy and inviting she couldn't resist spread-eagling on it. She closed her eyes and smoothed her arms up and down on the slick surface making 'angel wings' like she used to do in the snow.

"Ahem." Kevin cleared his throat. "Excuse me for intruding on what obviously is some native ritual, but I'm ready now."

Her face flushed at being caught. "This has got to be the biggest bed in the world."

"It is larger than most," Kevin informed, sitting down next to her.

"Remember in the old movies where a couple couldn't be shown in bed together unless they had one foot on the floor?" She spread her arms out wide. "I'll bet they couldn't 'do' anything in THIS bed with one foot on the floor."

He threw his head back and laughed. "You're right. There would be no way they could make...well, you know...in a bed this size." He laid down on his back, his hands behind his head. "You like old movies?"

"Yes. Movies today are too graphic when it comes to love scenes. It doesn't leave much to your imagination."

Kevin turned to look at her. "Don't you think even if one foot was on the floor that they didn't become...kind of 'involved'?"

"I don't think so." They both laughed at the thought, then trickled to a grin. "Sexual involvement is all in the mind anyway," she informed very clinical.

"Oh?"

"Yeah, mind over matter." She giggled. "I don't mind and you don't matter." She stared at him for a moment. "No, really, couldn't you play a scene like that and 'keep your cool'...I could," she insisted.

"Well, sure...I suppose if I really wanted to."

She grinned. "I'll bet you'd cave in at the first sight of bare skin above the knee."

"Put your money where your mouth is."

"You serious?" Her voice quivered a little, wondering what she was getting herself into.

"Put up or shut up," he told her emphatically, jumping up, unbuttoning his shirt and pulling it out of his trousers.

"Wha...what are you doing? I hadn't exactly thought about us stripping."

"I don't want to get my clothes wrinkled." He pulled his belt from the loops and eyed the panicked look on her face as he began to unzip his pants. "Come on," he urged, motioning for her to undress. "You won't go through with this, will you?" he teased.

Kara could never stand to be dared to do anything...but this?

He slowly started pushing his trousers down over his hips and when she saw about an inch of his white underwear, she yelled, "Wait!"

He stopped and studied her. "What's the matter? Can't

stand the heat?" he heckled.

"Don't be silly. You can't shock me. I was raised with four brothers, remember?" She tried to sound nonchalant, considering her heart was pumping blood to her head so fast it sounded like a thrashing machine. She nervously cleared her throat. "It...it's just that I thought we could do this with our clothes on. After all, we're just pretending—"

"Just as I thought," he cut in triumphantly, pulling his pants back up and fastening the waist, "you're chicken. If you don't have the guts to do it authentically...well then I guess I win."

Chicken? She hated to be called that. Her brothers used to goad her with that remark. "Okay, Mr. Cool, we'll see who turns chicken first." As she unhooked the halter strap around her neck, she thought of a relieving fact. "I agree this should be authentic...so we only strip down to our underwear. In those old movies they were never naked under all those blankets."

"Aww, what party poops," he joked, sitting on the edge of the bed to remove his shoes and socks. Laughing, he glanced up at her to make some comment about old movies, but whatever he was going to say immediately left his mind and his laugh dwindled to a lopsided, nervous twitch of his mouth.

Her dress had just swooshed to the floor around her feet and she stepped out of it and her shoes at the same time. She was wearing a matching set of ecru panties and strapless bra trimmed in a lighter shade of lace.

"Yee haw!" was all he could manage to say.

Trying to gain some sense of composure, he jumped up and turned his back on her as he shed himself of his trousers and laid them neatly across the bed. "Ahem...well...you...um...you have excellent taste in lingerie. I'll have to say that for you."

She laughed softly at his frustration. "Piece of cake," she told him. "I'll have this bet won before you even get through fiddling with trying to get the creases matched evenly in your pants." Was he always this fastidious with his clothes, she wondered, looking at her dress in a heap in the floor.

Still turned from her, she reached out and fluttered her fingers against his bare back, taking him completely by surprise.

His head whirled around so fast, he nearly snapped his neck. His hands went just as quickly to cover the front of his shorts.

"Holy cow, Kara, do you always sneak around like that?"

"Only during mating season. I like to catch up on the male species' latest tactics." She giggled, pointing to the mirror. "I saw you striking a pose and flexing your muscles. I'm afraid you'll have to do a little better than that to get me to lose my cool. Cute butt, though," she teased.

"Did anyone ever tell you, you had a smart mouth?"

"Many times." She patted the bed beside her. "Lay down, my darling," she said in a lilting 'old-movie' dialogue. "Remember one foot on the floor."

The bed was so wide, they were only able to hold hands. She smiled at him. "I don't think they had king size beds in old movies."

He rolled over and wrapped her in his arms.

"No, Kevin, don't! Remember I have heart trouble."

"Oh sure, play the 'I'm sickly' card." He lifted himself up on his elbow. "Give up?"

She pulled back and looked him in the eye, her voice barely a whisper. "One thing you need to know about me...I *never* give up."

"Okay, but we need a better strategy."

She smiled and turned on her stomach but still had a leg hung over the side. "One foot out, remember?"

"Oh, yeah. Well, let's see...you put your right foot out and I'll put my left...no, I'll turn just a little—"

"Wait, your knee is in my armpit. Let me scoot down—"

"Yeow! Watch your toe!"

They both got the giggles.

"This just can't be done," Kevin assured. "There is no way to even come close to making it with one foot out."

She thought a moment, then very quietly said, "If I show you how it can be done, will you concede the bet?"

"It can't be done," he reiterated strongly.

"I know a way," she returned just as strongly.

He let his breath out noisily. "Okay, okay, go ahead and show me, but remember, one foot out and one foot in but," he hesitated a second, "the bet was not to lose our cool."

She chuckled mischievously. "I'll not only show you how, but I'll show you who loses their cool first." She rose to a stand with one foot at the side of the bed, pulling him up with her on the same side. "Now, we lean one foot on the floor and put one foot on the bed."

"Standing up? That's not fair."

"Maybe I didn't make all the rules clear in the beginning," she said seductively, twining her arms around his neck. "We didn't decide exactly how much of our body had to be in the bed, nor..." she hooked a finger in the top of his jockey shorts and gave them a snap, "...did we say we had to be lying down," she finished, her lips brushing over his with butterfly kisses.

A moan escaped his throat as his arms clasped around her waist to draw her closer. His mouth descended to hers softly at first, then firm, then with an urgency that could not be denied, nor did she want to deny him. Ecstasy coursed through her veins and if she had ever doubted her feelings for him, she didn't now. She was definitely falling in love. *God give me strength to cope.*

"Kara," he whispered, his lips moist and warm against her ear. "I...I think I've lost the bet."

A satisfied smile crossed her lips. "I know you have."

CHAPTER SEVENTEEN

The drive to the farm was mostly silent except for an occasional sigh. Kara glanced at Kevin a few times and he at her, but otherwise she just stared out the window at the passing landscape.

As they turned into the lane toward her house, they both spoke at once.

"I was thinking…"

"You first," Kevin said.

"No, you go."

"I'll walk you to your door. We need to talk."

"I know. This was a crazy night. I'm sorry your car seats got wet."

Kevin chuckled. "That's the least of my concern."

"Yeah, mine too." She searched for words. "First, I want you to know I really like you and have had the most fun with you than I've had…I don't know…forever, but—"

"I hate 'buts', although I feel we are on the same page. Tonight *was* crazeee."

They reached the porch and patted the pets on the head that were very happy to see them.

"Go lie down," Kara warned them.

They, of course, did as she said.

"You certainly have a way with pets…and people," he said with a hint of sadness in his voice.

"Kevin, I want to apologize for my actions at your apartment. We shouldn't have turned what was just fun and games into something more serious. You know there can't be…"

"I know and that is what I was about to say." He thought for a moment, then, "I want you to know nothing would have gone any further. I respect you too much. I respect your faith, your illness…everything about you."

"What about your faith?"

"That's not a part of my life Kara, but that doesn't keep me from respecting yours."

"Kevin, just because you have stepped away from God doesn't mean He has forsaken you." She reached up and stroked his cheek. "Oh, Kevin, I wish I could convey how beautiful life really is with God by our side."

He smiled at her. "You are the most amazing woman I've ever known. You have everything to be depressed about yet you're so happy and just keep on keeping on. I don't know where your strength comes from…oh, don't answer that. I know you'll say God."

"Well, then I don't have to say anything more." She looked at him for a long moment. "Was that all you wanted to talk about?"

"No." He ran his fingers through his hair. "This is hard for me to say because I like you so well, but tonight showed me that I can't be trusted to be alone with you. I wanted to make love to you so badly, I nearly went out of my mind."

"I think I knew that and I really appreciate your being a gentleman. I certainly was not a lady and I agree; we should not do anything like that again."

"I do have feelings for you, but…"

"I also hate buts."

"I don't know anyone who is more fun."

She rolled her eyes toward him and noted his brows knitted with concern. "Do you want your face to freeze like that?"

He smiled and kissed her on the forehead. "Goodnight, Kara. Take care."

"You too. Again, sorry about tonight. I wish things…stuff hadn't happened."

"Aside from all that, nothing further was going to happen

anyway."

She raised her eyebrows. "Oh?"

"I didn't have protection."

She had to chuckle. "I take it you don't mean a gun."

He laughed out loud. "No, but a gun would have been a quicker mood changer."

"I'm sorry, Kevin, I didn't plan for this to happen. I know we carried things too far and…"

"I think we should not see each other for a while." He blurted it out so fast he had to catch his breath.

She sighed, her heart saddened. "I guess that would be best." She turned to go into the house, then turned back. "Oh, word of advice. It would be dumb of you to 'go all the way' with *anyone*…especially without, you know, a gun."

He laughed again. "Yes, counselor."

****

Although Kara kept herself very busy Saturday morning playing 'catch up' on paper work and 'clean up' on the living room, she was still saddened by the fact she felt she had lost her best friend. She also busied herself checking out everything in the Kids Haven to make sure it was ready for the inspector in a few days. Her mood lightened when she looked around and thought of it being filled with kids who needed a safe place to come to in troubled times.

The couple from church had also stopped by and was delighted with everything that had been accomplished. They had said they couldn't believe the Haven had been an old barn. They even picked out their room they would use to stay overnight in and assured Kara one of them would be there at all times.

Still Kevin kept creeping into her mind and not just that she would not be seeing him, but that he had given up on God. That saddened her even more. What had he told her once? 'Love meant losing'? Even though love between them could never be, she prayed he'd find love in his life. Everyone should have love in their heart.

She ran to the house, gave the pets a treat and took a cool shower and washed her hair. Monday was payday. Maybe she could work in a beauty shop appointment for a cut, a new hairdo. Maybe that would make her feel better. She doubted it. Money better spent on new carpet for the living room.

Sitting at her dressing table looking at herself in the mirror, she absently ran her fingers through her just-washed hair. Yeah, maybe if she scrimped on lunches, she could do both. She did need a haircut.

The ringing of the house phone caused her to nearly jump out of her skin. Not even looking at the caller I.D. she answered on the first ring hoping it would be Kevin.

"We're back!" came a friendly, familiar voice over the line. "What's wrong with your cell phone? It went straight to voice mail."

"Barb! Has it been two weeks already? I hardly knew you were gone," Kara teased laughingly. "I forgot to turn my cell back on from last night."

"Oh? What went on last night?" Barb's voice was dripping with sexual innuendoes.

"Nothing like that."

"A girl can hope, can't I?"

"Actually, I did have a sort of date with Kevin Michals. We went to a play in the park."

"Kevin Michals? The attorney?" Barb let out a snide chuckle. "Girl, no one has a 'sort of date' with Kevin Michals."

"Well, I did and that's all I'm going to say about it, except it rained us out."

"I see. Well since you didn't miss me, I'll be more than happy to take another two weeks."

"Forget that! I frankly couldn't survive another two weeks like these."

"That bad, huh?" Barb asked seriously, then brightly, "Nice to be missed though."

"Well you must feel *very* 'nice' then because you were definitely missed. But did you have a good time?"

"The goodest," Barb informed delightfully. "However, I think I will go away again if I can come home to some more gifts. Kara, the hanging table is simply beautiful and the plant—"

"What plant?"

"Oh, you don't know? Your 'sort of date', Kevin Michals

who was house sitting bought a beautiful plant for your table."

"So he gave you the plant. How thoughtful." Kara wanted to change the subject of Kevin so she said, "I thought you weren't going to be back until tomorrow."

"Missed you."

"Baloney."

"We needed to get things done here. Good news though, we came home to find a cleaning lady just finishing up on spit shining our new house. What a treat! That 'sort of' person thinks of everything. The house looks like it has been buffed, the refrigerator and cabinets are stocked with at least a month's supply of food."

"Gee."

"And if that weren't enough, there's a DVR hooked up to the bedroom TV and a stack of old romantic movies. He left a note telling us to use these as a 'guide line' and we'd have the best time of our lives."

"Gee again."

"Yeah, the cleaning lady said he came real early this morning and did all that. Isn't he positively decadent?"

"Positively." Kara's heart raced at the remembrance of her and Kevin's reenactment of an 'old movie' script.

"Well, gotta go," Barb announced abruptly, then whispered, "John's picking out a movie as we speak, so…" she let out an insidious chuckle, "…see you Monday," adding, "maybe."

Kara laughed. "No 'maybe', you creep."

CHAPTER EIGHTEEN

The sermon Sunday morning couldn't have been more appropriate. It was on love and forgiveness. Not just forgiving your fellow man, but forgiving yourself for 'leaving the flock' and going away from God. Just a whisper of His name brings Him back. You don't need a long, lengthy prayer. You don't need to confess anything—God already knows and is waiting to hear that whisper.

Kara could not help but think of Kevin and what made him 'leave the flock' so to speak. It dawned on her she knew very little about him personally. She knew he had a good heart. Look what he did for Barb and John and what he tried to do to help with her plumbing. She almost laughed thinking about that fiasco...but he did try. The only time she saw a really dark side was with her little neighbor boy, Aaron. That still puzzled her.

When she got home she made her weekly call to her mother. Her mom expected to hear from her on a regular basis. Like all moms, she worried about her being on her own.

"Mom, it's me."

"Yes, me. How you been?"

"Fine."

"Hmm, you don't sound fine."

"Why do you say that?"

"I know my only daughter and I can tell by the tone of your voice that everything is not 'fine'. Is it your heart?"

"In a way, but not like you think. Health-wise, I haven't had much problem. It's heart problems of another nature."

"And?"

"I met a man I actually developed feelings for."

"Oh, honey, I was afraid that would happen someday. Be careful. "

"Mom! I know. Jack told him about my heart and he's very understanding. He knows I won't...can't have any kind of relationship beyond friendship."

"Then what's the problem?"

"I think he has feelings for me...beyond friendship and so he's asked not to see me alone anymore."

"Alone? Did something happen?"

"No, Mom, of course not." She let her breath out noisily. "I shouldn't have told you. It's just that I've never had these feelings before and I don't know how to handle the situation. Now you'll worry even more."

Her mother chuckled. "Like I could worry more than I do."

"Well, don't worry. This will probably pass. We have absolutely nothing in common, but I've had a good time with him, just fun stuff. He's a good man down deep but he's lost his faith in God."

"Oh, dear. You don't want that."

"I know but I don't want that for him either. He was raised in the church, but something happened in his adult life that turned him against God. I wish I could say or do something—"

"Honey, you have enough on your plate. It's sweet of you to care, but you shouldn't be worried about saving someone. You need to worry about your health."

"I know you're right, Mom. Let's change the subject. The Kids Haven is ready for inspection and then I'll apply for a license and we'll be ready to open it to those in need."

"Have I told you how proud of you I am?"

"Only hundreds of times." Kara laughed. "You're the greatest mom in the world."

"I love you, child. Pray for guidance with your other 'heart' problem."

"I will and I'm so grateful to have you for a mom. Call you soon."

"Okay, sweetie. Again, don't worry about your friend. You know God has a way of sneaking back into someone's life when they least expect it...even without the help of Kara Peters."

"I know, Mom. Love you."

"Love you, too."

Talking to her mom always made Kara feel so much better about everything. Even at her darkest, worrisome moments, her mom could put things in perspective and 'make it all better'.

Just as she closed her cell phone, she heard a vehicle coming up the lane. It sounded a lot like Jack's old pickup truck.

She walked out on the porch and saw that it was indeed Jack. He got out and the dogs ran to him, jumping up on his body. "Get these animals off me!"

"Come on, guys. It's only grumpy old Jack." The dogs ran back to her. "If you don't change your tone, I can sic them on you again."

"Shut up. I could be out on the golf course instead of delivering a clothes dryer to you."

"I didn't order a clothes dryer."

"Yeah, I was told you'd say that."

"By whom?"

Kevin stepped out of the passenger side. "By me."

"Kevin? What are you doing here?"

"Helping Jack deliver a clothes dryer."

"Oh, no you don't. I'll not accept this from you."

Kevin poked Jack in the shoulder. "Told you. She's holding out for jewelry."

"Yeah, her old aunt taught her well."

Kara glared at them. "You are both in a heap of trouble."

Jack ignored her. "Come on Kevin, let's get that old piece of junk out of the house before we take this off the truck."

"Both of you stay out of my house," she called out, pointing toward Jack and Kevin, "Pooch, Scooter attack!!!"

As the dogs ran to their prey, Kevin took two donut holes out of the sack he was holding and the dogs stopped in their tracks, bowed their heads in prayer and waited for their treat.

"Amazing," Kevin said in awe, then turned to Jack. "Have you seen these animals do that before?"

"Oh, yeah. Praying balls of fur." He looked the dogs over.

"Where'd this short/long one come from?"

Kara smiled smugly. "God sent him."

Jack turned to Kevin. "God has a funny sense of humor. That's where Kara gets it."

The guys sidestepped Kara and went into the house and proceeded unhooking an old dryer.

Jack pinched his nostrils. "P.U. This smells like it's burnt."

"It is," Kevin answered matter-of-factly.

"How did it—"

Kevin started to explain but Kara stopped him. "It's no one's fault. It's old, so why don't you two just get out of here and take that new dryer back." She turned to Kevin. "I will not have you buying me a dryer."

"It's the least I can do."

"No, the least you can do is leave…with Jack *and* the dryer."

"Hey, you two, I've got a tee time with my name on it. Let's get crackin'."

Knowing she was not going to win, she stepped aside and graciously bowed to them. "Knock yourselves out." She then promptly went to the living room.

In a very short time, the old dryer was out, loaded to be taken to the dump and the new one in.

After calming down a bit, she returned to the kitchen and couldn't help but admire the new dryer.

Jack patted her on the shoulder. "You know, you could say thank you."

"I'm sorry. Thank you."

"Not to me. Kevin."

"Thank you, Kevin." She ventured just a short glance toward him, then dropped her gaze to the floor. "I thought we were not going to see each other again."

"Alone. I said alone."

Jack frowned and turned quickly to Kevin. "What? What are you talking about, not seeing each other alone." He poked Kevin in the chest. "You been alone with Kara? What did you do to her? You dirty so-and-so, you did something, didn't you? I told you I'd kill you if you *ever*—"

"Guys! I can hear you, you know. I'm right here." Kara

pulled them apart. "He didn't do anything to me."

"What'd you do to him?" Jack looked her in the eye. "What'd you do to him that he would buy you an expensive present? Your brothers are going to wipe me off the map when they find out—"

"Stop it, Jack. I didn't do anything to Kevin and he didn't do anything to me. Besides it would be none of your business."

"Oh don't you dare tell me it's none of my business. I've been delegated to—"

"I know, I know, Jack. I'm sorry. I appreciate you. I really do, but *nothing* happened for you to be concerned about."

Jack calmed down a bit. "Better not be. I'll let it go for now, but if I ever—"

"You'll have to overlook Jack's tirades, Kevin. He doesn't play well with others." Kara gave Jack a warning glance.

Jack shrugged and looked around the kitchen. "Like what you've done. You got a beer in that thing you call a refrigerator."

Kara squinted her eyes at him.

"Kidding. Can't you take a joke?"

She looked at Kevin. "See what I told you. Skinny legged, thinks he's funny."

Kevin smiled. "Come on Jack. I think we've enjoyed as much 'fun' as we can stand for one day." He then looked at Kara sympathetically. "Sorry for upsetting you. I just felt bad about the dryer and thought I'd help out."

"Thanks, Kevin, and I really mean that."

"See you in court?"

"Not if I can help it."

****

If she had her way, Kara would insist Mondays be stricken from the week and banished into never-never land. They were only good for problems. As soon as she walked into her office, she received a call from the rehabilitation center informing her Wynona Becker was not reporting for her sessions.

After calling Wynona and insisting she be ready in exactly one hour, Kara made arrangements for a sitter for Teresa, grabbed her purse and sack lunch and out the door she went to personally escort Wynona to the center.

It had been slow going, but Kara could see some progress since she first took the case. At least now Teresa's diet seemed to be adequate, she was always clean and while her clothes were certainly not the best, they were suitable. When Wynona wasn't appeasing her love affair with the bottle, she did make a concerted effort to take good care of Teresa and herself.

Kara's mind dwelled on little Teresa again, so wise for so young. If only the child would unleash the demon that was keeping her from talking. A lump sprang to her throat and, as if the old Buick was reading her mind, it instinctively turned into the small shopping center that just happened to have a toy store. Kara knew it was unprofessional, but there was no force that could stop her…not even the fact her cash was limited. Her haircut could wait. Right now there was a very important doll to be purchased.

She found the perfect one with a string to pull to make it say, "I love you, mommy," or, "Can I have a cookie?" or, "Hi, my name is Penny. What's yours?" Kara casually counted out the money like she had it to burn, finding it hard to keep from grinning ear to ear thinking about the look on Teresa's face when she gave the doll to her.

Fifteen minutes later Kara was viewing that look and it was worth a million haircuts. When the doll said, "I love you, mommy," Teresa hugged it tight against her chest and rocked back and forth. It did Kara's heart good to know that Teresa had obviously learned to rock a baby by being rocked herself. At least she had been cuddled and loved at some time during her young life.

As soon as the sitter arrived, Kara explained again to Teresa they would be back in a few hours and the little girl, although showing sadness, seemed to understand the situation. Teresa motioned for her mother to wait, then pulled the string on her doll until it repeated, "I love you, mommy."

"I love you, too, baby," Wynona said, her voice cracking hoarsely both from emotion as well as too many cigarettes.

As they drove to the center, Kara instigated the conversation. "I wish you wouldn't be so reluctant to go to these sessions, Wynona. Look at it this way. This is a giant step up, a new beginning for you and Teresa."

"I need a drink. Just one."

"No, you don't, Wynona. Everything's going to be okay."

"I ain't had none for a long time, Ms. Peters. I'm hurtin' bad. Maybe if I could have just one…if you would just loan me some money 'til…no I don't s'pose you would." She was nearly in tears now. "Sometimes I'm so ashamed of myself."

Kara listened patiently. She had heard this story many times from many different people, but each one thought it was only happening to them; that there was no one else in the world suffering quite as much as they were.

"Wynona, have you ever gone to church?"

"Did once. Went to Sunday school with a neighbor girl when I was young."

"Why'd you stop?"

"Don't have the right clothes."

"I don't think Jesus cares how you dress."

"Jesus. They gave me a picture of Jesus. I think I still got it somewhere. He looked like a nice man."

Kara chuckled. "Yes, Wynona, he's a very nice man. Did you know he's the son of God?"

"I think they told me that when I got the picture."

"You and Teresa should find a church near you and go. I think you'd like it."

"I don't know. I ain't got much learnin' and can't read that Bible they got."

Wynona was very quiet for a long moment and Kara became concerned. "Something bothering you?"

"This guy I know was supposed to come by the house last night. I only had five dollars to my name. He said he would give me a few bucks if I'd…" She picked at the chipped polish on her fingernails.

"What guy?"

Wynona shrugged. "Some guy. I got nervous waiting for him so Teresa and I walked down to the corner store. She told me we were out of milk. She's better at keepin' track of food in the house. I forget sometimes. I had enough food stamps for the milk but I bought a pack of cigarettes with my last cent, then Tom…the guy," she quickly corrected, "never showed."

Tom? Did she say Tom? Kara couldn't be sure, but Teresa's father's name was Tom and he could very well be the 'guy'.

"Who did you say, Wynona?"

"Just a guy. He was gonna bring a bottle over and we was gonna watch a little TV—"

"Bring a bottle over. Wynona!" Kara's voice dropped disappointedly.

"I know what you're gonna say. I've said it to myself already. I told you I was ashamed of myself." She stared out the window. "Some ways I'm glad he didn't show, others I'm not so sure." She looked directly at Kara. "You understand, don't ya? You surely got somebody you think about a lot."

Kara's mind instantly pictured Kevin and could almost feel his arms around her, but she remained quiet until they reached their destination.

"Here we are." She squeezed Wynona's hand as a token of friendship. "Be selective, Wynona. You could have so much going for you."

Wynona laughed nervously. "I ain't gonna 'mount to anything."

"Who told you that? The 'guy'?"

Wynona remained silent.

Kara looked deep into the young woman's eyes, repeating, "Just be particular about the men in your life, not just for yourself, but for Teresa. You've got to know you're teetering on the brink of losing your child."

Wynona hung her head. "I know that, Ms. Peters."

"You can call me anytime you need me. I don't want to see anything bad happen to you or Teresa."

Wynona fidgeted nervously. "What could you do? You're just a woman. I mean what if I was needin' a...a...strong person."

"Wynona, has someone hurt you?" She remembered there were times when Wynona suffered from unexplained bruises.

"No...no, I was just what if'n."

"Well, I would bring someone 'strong' with me. I would take you to Women's Strength where you would be safe from all harm and I would take Teresa somewhere safe. There's a *lot* I can do, but the main thing is I want you to know you can count on me." Kara handed Wynona a card. "Here's a hot line to call in case of an emergency if I'm not available."

Wynona made a swipe at her damp eyes. "Thanks, Ms. Peters. I don't know why you're so good to us."

"Because you're worth it. Remember that, Wynona," Kara stressed. "Be proud of yourself and others will be proud of you and don't forget, God loves you."

"Me?" She gave Kara a puzzled look. "How could God love me after all the bad stuff I've done."

"He's in the business of forgiving, but you've got to forgive yourself first and, of course, He'd like you to stop the 'bad stuff' for your own sake. Find a church, Wynona, for Teresa to learn about Jesus and all the good He can bring into your lives. You don't have to be able to read the Bible. There will be others there who will teach the Bible to you."

Wynona took a deep breath and straightened. "Guess I'd better get in there and get rehabilitated," she said spiritedly. "You comin'?"

"You betcha!"

CHAPTER NINETEEN

It had been a long morning and she was ready for lunch by the time she dropped Wynona off at her home. The good thing was Wynona promised she would continue the meetings on her own with Kara dropping by occasionally to see how she was progressing.

Teresa walked Kara to her car and gave her a big hug and kiss as a 'thank you' for the doll. Kara hugged her back for a long time, having to force herself to let go. If there was one thing she learned in this profession, and wholeheartedly agreed to, was every child had the right to a home, a family and the chance to grow to his or her potential; and to have the security that comes from feeling safe and belonging. She vowed Teresa and all children she came in contact with would have those privileges if it was the last thing she did on this earth. She had faith with God's guidance, she could very well accomplish this.

As she wended her way through the downtown traffic, the prospects of eating a sack lunch alone was a little too dreary for her today. She felt down in the dumps and needed a friend…she needed Kevin. She felt she did not properly thank him for the dryer. A broad grin spread over her face as a brilliant idea popped into her head. An office picnic. Kevin's office would be public enough as to not compromise their pledge to not be alone together.

She stopped by a nearby Stop and Shop and picked out a

ninety-nine cent bottle of sour grape juice. It looked festive enough, kind of like wine. Still smiling, she quickly made it to Kevin's office.

The receptionist did a double take as Kara scurried by her, dragging a tattered blanket she had grabbed from the trunk of her car.

"Did you have an appointment?"

"Oh, I'm not here on business, just lunch."

Kara held the rumpled sack containing one peanut butter sandwich, an apple and two Fig Newtons under one elbow while under the other arm was an emergency flare...the closest thing she had to create a 'candlelight' lunch.

The receptionist raised her brows. "I'll see if he's in."

"Oh, I'm in for Ms. Peters," Kevin said as he stood at his office door, trying to stifle a laugh.

Kara gently nudged him back into his office and closed the door with her foot.

Kevin let out a startled, "Wow!" as she proceeded to spread the fare on the floor in front of his desk. "You're not going to light that thing," he questioned when she put the flare in the center of the blanket.

"It's only for show. I hope you didn't have other plans for lunch."

"And miss all this? No way." He laughed and seated himself on the floor.

"Glasses." She looked around the room. "I need two glasses."

"Coffee cups in the top file drawer." He nodded her in the right direction then leaned back on his hands and watched as she busied herself in preparation of the 'feast'.

She tore the one napkin from her sack in two and put the pieces down as placemats, then set the cups in front. Thinking she had brought wine, a dour look spread over Kevin's face when he read the label, but he obliged by pouring while she cut the apple in half with his pearl-handled letter opener. Each was treated with a Fig Newton and half a sandwich.

"Voila!" she announced, plopping down at her spot and picking her cup up in a toast. "Say something very profound and lawyer-ish."

He thought a moment then clicked his cup to hers. "To the lips and over the gums. Look out stomach, her it comes."

"If that's all you got, I could have went to Jack's for lunch." She laughed, taking a cautious sip and puckering unmercifully.

Kevin's swallow almost refused to go down but when it did, his lips tightened in a straight line. "I may never speak again."

"It does have a bit of a bite." She put her cup down in lieu of the sandwich. "I apologize. Your toast was more appropriate than I thought. I should have sprung for the more expensive grape juice."

Half way through her sandwich she noticed he wasn't eating his. He was just leaning back and watching her. Her face reddened at his scrutiny. "The rest of the lunch tastes okay...really."

"I'm not all that hungry...I'd rather look at you."

"Gee, I'm flattered."

"No, I'm flattered...flattered that you would go to all this trouble."

"This was trouble?"

They both laughed, sincerely amused with each other and not knowing why.

"Why are you really here, Kara?"

She gave a slight shrug. "Wanted to thank you again for the dryer. You really did not need to do that, you know."

"I know. I wanted to." He smiled at her again. "But why are you *really* here?"

She started gathering up the 'picnic'. "You're not happy I'm here. I'll go."

"Not happy you're here? Are you kidding? You're a delight to be with. My face hurts from laughing. I have so much fun with you. I can't remember this much joy since—"

Kara looked up to see why he had stopped talking and saw a troubled, pensive look settle into his features. "Since when, Kevin?"

He shook his head and snapped out of his trance. "Since...I don't know when," he finished lamely. "Since I was last with you."

She felt he was keeping something inside that was troubling him, so in an attempt to lighten the mood, Kara suggested, "Take another drink. That should keep you from laughing for a while."

His smile brought a softening to his features which still held a touch of sadness. They sat in silence for a long moment.

"Penny for your thoughts," she finally whispered.

"Penny? How cheap can you get?" he teased.

She was thrilled to see his good humor returning. "The drink I brought sort of tells you how cheap I can get."

He laughed at that as he stood to help her with the blanket. "I'll admit the drink did leave a lot to be desired, but the company made up for it."

"Really?"

"Really." He pulled her into his arms, blanket and all, and pressed his lips to her forehead, repeating, "Really."

"Do you treat all your lunch dates this way?"

"Only during mating season."

"Barb said you were decadent. She's right."

"Barb?" He backed off and looked puzzled.

"Yes. She told me about the old romantic movies you left in their bedroom."

"Oh, that." His ears turned red.

"Yes, that. Wonder what made you think of old movies in the bedroom?"

He let his breath out noisily. "Kara, you're driving me crazy. Of course I think about our acting out old movies, but we've agreed we can never do anything like that again."

"I know. We were wrong. You are *not* one of my crazy brothers I used to play pranks on. We should have never put ourselves in such a precarious situation and I *am* so very sorry for my part in it. Believe me I've prayed to God about it, but we can still be friends, can't we?"

He turned and rubbed the back of his neck. "I don't know what in the world you see in me."

"I don't either...a big old ugly lout like you. But with all your faults, I still like you."

He turned back to face her. "And I like you. That's my problem. I like you very much."

She nervously gathered up the rest of her stuff, gave him a friendly kiss on the cheek, and said, "Thanks for putting up with my less-than-gourmet lunch."

He touched his cheek where her lips had been. "Do you ever regret we made that pact not to—"

"I can't think about regrets, Kevin." Walking to the door, she turned back. "I've got to go." She wanted to end on a light note. "You might be able to play around all day, but I've got business to attend to."

"Kara...I..." He reached for her.

"Oh, you needn't thank me for lunch," she cut in, not knowing what he was going to say. "But if you insist on paying me back, come over tonight and help me and Jack paper one wall in the bedroom."

"Kara..."

"Seven would be fine. You can keep me and Jack from hurting each other."

"Kara! Listen to me. I need to talk to you."

"We can talk tonight."

"Not at your place. It's such a madhouse most of the time and with Jack there what I have to say to you would not be feasible. Let me take you to dinner someplace tomorrow night."

"Not a good idea...for more reasons than one. I'm on the beeper this week. You know, Child Protective Service Worker Investigator. We have to do it twice a year for a week. This is my week so I'm on call after seven thirty every evening for the entire night. It would be better if I stayed around home in case I had to leave on an emergency." She looked at him and grinned mischievously. "Besides, you wanted to learn how to hang paper."

Kevin sighed and opened the door for her. "I don't recall saying that. I must have been under duress, but okay. What should I bring to get this paper hung?"

"Coney dogs. Bring several. Jack's a really big eater."

He frowned. "Chili dogs help paper walls?"

She shrugged. "Works for me."

123

CHAPTER TWENTY

The next few days were just about as perfect as Kara could hope for. With Barb back at the office, Kara found time to sneak in extra visits with Teresa to play with her and wash the little girl's hair. She fixed it with pretty barrettes she had bought at the Dollar Store. Yes, it had been a great week, she reflected while humming her favorite hymn. The words she loved were, "Jesus, Jesus, there's just something about that name." Yes, life was good.

Of course, Kevin's help with wallpapering still amused her. She smiled inwardly recalling the strip that refused to stick and fell across Kevin's head while he was on the stepstool. She was still a little miffed at Jack for bailing out on them after eating his fill of Coney dogs, saying he had to meet up with his bowling team. Oh well, that's Jack. At least he helped measure and cut the strips before he left.

She was surprised after all the mishaps that Kevin still agreed to come to the farm to look over the contract for her license to operate Kids Haven. He never did talk to her so she did not know what he had on his mind. She had offered to pop some corn so they could relax, watch some TV and have their talk, but he said he had to go but would be back in a few days to go over the contract.

She glanced up at the clock on the wall. It was about time for him to get here.

Her musings were interrupted by the dogs barking.

"Wanna see my new bike?" came a small excited voice through the back door.

"Aaron!" She was delighted to see his little smudged nose pressed against the screen. She put the contract back on the table and walked outside.

"Look at these!" Aaron pointed at the red reflectors on the wheels, then pushed the two-wheeler as fast as his little legs would go. "See how they sparkle when I run fast!" He squealed joyously causing the dogs to jump and leap along with him.

Kara laughed and shared his glee. "Why don't you get on it and pedal?"

"I don't know how to ride it yet," he returned disappointedly, explaining, "Mommy never learned how so I have to wait until Uncle Bill comes over Sunday to teach me."

Kara's heart went out to the little boy. He was so happy and well-adjusted she sometimes forgot he had no father...only 'uncles' who came in and out of his widowed mother's life.

"Maybe I could show you," she offered, bragging, "I used to be a champion bike rider. Why, I could beat my brothers by a mile."

Aaron jumped on one leg, eager to get to his first lesson when Kevin pulled into the drive. The dogs immediately ran toward the car while Smokey, in her cat-like manner, sat on the porch and watched.

"Oh, no," Aaron moaned. "Here comes your grouchy friend." His bottom lip stuck out in a pout. "Now I won't get to learn."

"Not necessarily," Kara said just above a whisper. "We're going to play a little pretend game," she explained quickly, waving to Kevin as he approached trying to push the dogs away. "Play like I don't know how either. That way, Kevin can teach us both."

Aaron giggled and clasped his hands, clearly loving the mystery of it all.

"Kevin," Kara called out, "you're just in time. We've been trying to figure out how to ride Aaron's new bike."

Kevin surveyed the duo speculatively but without enthusiasm. "You don't know how to ride a bike?" he asked

Kara.

"It's been so many years since..." That was not a lie. She had not ridden a bike for a long time.

"That's something you never forget," Kevin reminded.

"Well, exceptions to every rule."

She could tell his heart wasn't in it, but he set his briefcase down on the porch and took hold of the handle bars. "Okay, Kara, pay attention—"

"Ohhh, I have to go to the bathroom." Another true statement. She really did have to go. "You can show Aaron first."

"Can't his dad show him?" he yelled to her as she entered the house.

"I don't have a dad," Aaron said matter-of-factly. "He's in heaven with Jesus."

Kevin felt a frustrating tug at his heart. This was the last thing he wanted to be doing, but there was no way out of it so he might as well explain the tricks of riding to the boy. It was all he could do to put his arm around the little boy to hold him on the bike...the memories were painful, but at the same time there was something about the smell of a child's freshly shampooed hair that took Kevin back many years. Back to another little boy.

"Now, you try it alone," he instructed bluntly, snapping his mind back to the present. "Remember what I told you. When you feel yourself falling to one side, turn your wheel in that direction and keep pedaling." He let his breath out noisily when the boy tipped over. "Hold it! Don't put your foot down, Aaron, or you'll hurt yourself real bad." He helped the boy up and straightened the bike out. "Try it again. And keep peddling."

Within minutes, Aaron had the trick mastered...almost. Kara watched from the back door. She saw that Aaron was a little shaky, but what he lacked in skill he more than made up in sheer guts. She also saw Kevin smiling proudly as he watched the boy riding big circles around the huge oak tree.

"Atta boy. Just keep doing what you're doing. You've got it made, but," he cautioned, "don't get too cocky until you've mastered stopping a little better."

He left the boy and turned toward Kara on the porch. "That

kid's pretty smart for his age."

"Yeah, he is."

"Are you ready for your lesson?"

"Let him ride a little longer. This is so nice of you, Kevin."

"No problem. You got the contract?"

"It's on the kitchen table. Come on in."

Just then her beeper went off and after answering the call, her complete demeanor changed. Kevin watched a very uptight Kara throw things out of her purse in search of her car keys. Upon finding them, she breathlessly slung the strap over her shoulder.

"I've got to go, Kevin. Just take the contract with you and get back to me." She was running in circles. "I have an emergency. Tell Aaron he has to go home now."

"Hey, calm down," Kevin urged, taking hold of her shoulders. "Where's the fire?"

"Let go, Kevin. I've got to go…NOW!" Her eyes were glazed with deep concern. "It…it's the Becker house…Teresa… If anything's happened to that child." Her voice quivered on the verge of sobbing.

"Get hold of yourself, Kara!" Kevin gave her a gentle shake. "Did they give you any details?"

"A…a neighbor, I think, called. They heard screams for help and things being shattered and," she broke down, "oh, dear God, please let Teresa be safe."

"Kara, you have to be clinical about this. Go by the rules. You need to call for police protection."

"Rules!" She jerked away from him. "I don't have time for rules. I don't have time to wait for the police. She could be hurt."

"Oh, dear, Kara. You're even more attached to her than I thought." Kevin's eyes rolled in dazed exasperation, his voice dropping with disappointment. "You're just asking for heartbreak."

She whirled on him, her nerves clearly at the breaking point. "At least I have a heart to be broken. You don't have any attachments or feelings for little children. You won't *let* yourself love anyone."

They stared at each other across the sudden absolute silence, making her heartbeat sound like thunder. Finally she broke down and sobbed. She had been thoughtless and hurt him and she hated herself for that.

"Kevin…" She immediately reached for him and wanted to apologize but couldn't find anything to say that could take back her harsh words or erase the troubled, hurt expression on his face.

"You're right." He barely raised his voice above a whisper. "I don't expect you to understand."

Her body trembled as she fled out the door. Kevin was right behind her after grabbing up the contract and snatching his briefcase from the porch.

"Kara," he called to her retreating back, "don't leave so upset!"

At that very moment his voice was drowned out by the loud honking blare of an air horn on a gravel truck hurrying along the highway in front of Kara's lane. Kevin looked up to see Aaron speeding uncontrollably down the drive toward the path of the truck. He dropped his briefcase on the ground.

Five years were suddenly erased from his life and he was back again to that horrible day.

"Bobby!" Kevin ran as fast as he could toward the boy. He snatched Aaron off the bike just before it crashed into the side of the moving vehicle. "Bobby, Bobby," Kevin sobbed, cradling Aaron in his arms.

Frightened brown eyes looked up at him bewildered. "I'm Aaron," the boy said shakily.

By that time the driver had the truck stopped and was running over to them, brows knitted in concern. "Is he hurt?"

Kara was at their side checking Aaron for contusions or broken bones. "He…he appears to be fine," she answered, her own self a bit dazed.

Kevin stiffened and looked at Aaron as if seeing him for the first time. "Are you okay?"

Aaron nodded his head and wrapped his arms around Kevin's neck, giving him a big hug. "I'm sorry," the little boy said in a quivery voice. "Am I in trouble for not practicing stopping more?"

Kevin pulled the boy's arms from around his neck and stood up to retrieve the crumpled bike. "Everything's fine," he told the truck driver. "You can go on your way now. I'll take care of the bike."

The driver gave Aaron one last going over and seeing he could do nothing more, left.

Aaron stuck his thumb in his mouth and leaned into Kara for comfort while he looked disappointedly at his bicycle.

"I'll see that he gets a new one," Kevin informed in a calm, impersonal voice. "And, Aaron, you're not in trouble." He turned to Kara. "Can you take the time to see that his mother knows what happened?"

"Yes." Kara's eyes tried to capture his but he wouldn't look at her. "Bobby must have been someone very close to you," she said, saddened with sympathy.

Kevin's breathing became labored. "My…my son. He was about Aaron's age." His voice was distant, his eyes glancing downward. "Beth, my wife, was pedaling home from the grocery store on her bike. Bobby was sitting behind her." His words were spoken in a monotone. "I was watching them come down the street, laughing and having such a…a…good time." He faltered, swallowed hard and found his voice again. "This car came out of nowhere. I tried to make them hear, but they were laughing so loud. I ran as fast as I could."

Kara reached her hand out to him, but he turned away. "I'm sorry. This is all my fault."

"No, it isn't," Kevin snapped harshly more to himself for dredging up painful memories. "Just forget it." He retrieved his briefcase from the yard and turned toward his car.

"I can't forget it. I tricked you into teaching Aaron to ride his bike."

At those words, Kevin turned around to face her. "What do you mean?"

"I thought if I forced you to spend time with Aaron, you would change your mind about children." Tears welled. "Oh, Kevin, I'm such a fool…a selfish fool. I wanted you to love everything I loved. I have always had the feeling that you had been hurt badly sometime in your life, but I had no idea as to the extent. I was so quick to judge you heartless, I never once stopped to think…" She hung her head. "It's not like me to judge anyone, Kevin." She looked back at him, tears streaming down her cheeks. "I care for you. I am so sorry—"

"Stop it!" Kevin blurted. "Just leave me alone, Kara. Until I met you, I had all those memories buried and my life was finally running smoothly again. No surprises. No heartaches. Then you came along."

"Kevin, please." She followed right behind him.

He walked to his car and got in, turning to her one last time. "Forget about me, Kara," he pleaded softly, but firmly. "When I lost Beth and Bobby, my world ended and I thought I would *never* let myself love someone that much again. Then there you are. Someone I could deeply care about but can't have. I either lose the ones I love or can't have the ones I could love. Where was your God when all that happened?"

She put her hand on his shoulder. "*Our* God is right where He has always been...by our side to help us through hardships."

He shook his head. "I'm happy you believe. I just don't see it." With that he started his car and drove away, leaving Kara assailed with terrible regrets and a wretched ache in her heart.

CHAPTER TWENTY ONE

Kara came to her senses enough to heed Kevin's advice and 'follow the rules', calling for a patrolman to escort her to the Becker house. When they arrived they found Teresa sponging off her mother's bloody face with a washcloth. Wynona's clothes were torn and her wrists bruised from an obvious struggle.

Since Wynona and Teresa were the only two people left in the rubble of broken chairs and lamps, there was no one to tell Kara exactly what happened since Teresa couldn't talk and Wynona wouldn't.

After the ambulance took Wynona to the hospital, Kara dismissed the police officer, telling him she had everything under control. It was late and Teresa was so frightened Kara didn't have the heart to leave her with strangers, so she packed a few things in a sack, loaded her up in Old Betsy and took her home with her. She knew it was unethical, but it was the weekend and Teresa would be much better off with her. If she was called out on another emergency, she was sure Aaron's mother would look after Teresa for her.

****

The weekend passed much too quickly. Kara felt if she had a little more time with Teresa, she might get through to her. The little girl seemed delighted to play with the animals and Aaron took to her instantly. Her refusal to speak did not cause one problem with communication between the two as they sat in Sunday school. Teresa gave Kara the picture of an angel she colored, which Kara taped to the refrigerator door. That brought a big smile on Teresa's face. The little girl tucked the other picture she colored into the sack with her other belongings.

"For your mother?"

Teresa nodded and smiled up at Kara.

The child's favorite thing had been riding in Old Betsy so they took a trip to get an ice-cream cone. When the car backfired, sputtered and died at an intersection in town, Teresa laughed so hard she nearly dropped her cone. Kara did her magic under the hood and they were soon off on another adventurous drive through the country.

Even though she was enjoying her time with Teresa, her heart was still broken over Kevin. Her thoughts suddenly grew serious. She would love to have a child of her own but, unfortunately, she knew that would never happen. Kevin had confessed she was someone he could care about, but can't have. He was right, of course, but try to tell her heart that.

Kara noticed Teresa looking at her with sad eyes. The little girl kissed her finger and touched it to Kara's cheek.

"Thank you, sweetie. I'm okay. I was just thinking about things that made me a little sad for a moment, but," she smiled at the girl, "you make me happy."

Teresa patted her on the arm and then pointed upward.

"Yes, Teresa, I know Jesus will make us happy." She patted Teresa on the arm. "Did you have fun at church today?"

The little girl nodded her head with enthusiasm.

"Well, we'll see if you can go again or maybe your mom will go to a church near where you live."

Teresa shook her head no, then pointed to Kara.

"I'd love that, but it isn't possible for you to go with me every time."

They drove in silence for a couple of miles, then Kara asked, "Your mom will love the picture you colored for her. I'm going to have to take you home early in the morning so I can get to work on time."

Teresa nodded her head but still she looked sad and it broke

Kara's heart.

****

After mother and daughter were reunited Monday morning, Wynona gave Kara some cockamamie story about getting dizzy and falling into the furniture, but Kara had no time to press the issue today. She had other cases to attend to.

By the time she dragged home that evening, she felt her shoulders sag with the weight of responsibility as she heaved her bulging briefcase onto the table. She wished her 'magic fingers' could solve all the sadness she saw in her profession. While she was wishing, why not throw in a wish or two for things to work out for her and Kevin to remain friends. There was no denying her feelings for him. She also knew it would be hard to be 'just friends', but she wanted that anyway. She missed him. She missed the fun they shared, the laughter. He made her happy.

She sighed and said a prayer for forgiveness for the hurt she caused Kevin and hoped he could someday see how sorry she was. Her prayer was interrupted by Pooch and Scooter scratching at the door.

"Sorry guys. My mind was somewhere else." She opened the door and let them in for their treat. Smokey jumped in ahead of them. Kara laughed. "Cats are a little bossy, huh?" she said to the dogs. They all, of course, bowed their heads before she handed them the snack.

After letting them back out and giving them fresh water, she got herself a can of soda and sat down to thumb through the day's mail, tossing the 'occupant' junk in the trash. Her eyes fixed excitedly on a letter from her mother. She couldn't open it fast enough. She smiled and marveled at the fact that her mother still wrote letters, which was almost a dying art, but her mother felt it was more 'personal'. While reading, she let out an audible "yippee!" and ran out to the porch to tell the animals.

"Mom's coming this weekend." The pets stood up and wagged their tails expectantly. "My brother Paul is driving her down in his new pickup for Labor Day weekend." She hugged Pooch around the neck. "Mom's coming for three whole days!"

Oh, how she needed a heart to heart talk with her mom. Her

mother could always make things seem better and she needed her mom's down-to-earth advice right now on how to deal with her feelings for Kevin.

****

The week went rather well despite the fact she kept a watchful eye out for Kevin everywhere she went. She thought about calling him to inquire about the license contract, but didn't. She knew how thorough he was with business so she felt she should just wait it out and prayed she would hear from him soon. She practiced words to say to him to apologize again, but the right ones just wouldn't come. Her mom would probably know the right thing to do.

Her brother Paul and mother Jenny surprised Kara by being at her house when she arrived home Friday evening. They had purchased fried chicken along the way and supper was waiting on the table when she walked in.

"Oh, Mom," Kara greeted, giving the gray-haired woman a big hug and kiss. "What a sight for sore eyes!"

"And what about me?" Paul cut in, grabbing her for a hug himself.

Kara laughed, giving him a kiss. "I'm not going to tell you where YOU make me sore...it's not my eyes."

"Watch your smart mouth," he cautioned brotherly, "or I'll go back home and not help you fix up this fire trap."

"It's not a fire trap!"

"Jack told us about the dryer," Paul countered. "It's a fire trap."

"Oh...that...that was—"

"A fire," her brother stated flatly.

"Ahhh, just like old times," her mother reminisced, adding, "I told him to bring his work clothes because you would have a ton of things for him to do."

Kara eyed her brother suspiciously. "Jack. You've been talking to Jack?"

Paul grinned. "I called him to see if we could get together while I'm here and your name came up in conversation. Your name, your car, your house—"

"I'll just bet they did," Kara returned hotly. "Jack was a tattletale when we were kids and he still is."

"Now, now," Jenny cut in, "Jack was only looking out for your welfare." She patted Kara on the arm. "We've been admiring what you've done to the kitchen, dear, but the bedroom wallpaper..." Her voice dropped pathetically. "You must have been getting tired or something."

Kara smiled. "A...uh...friend helped with that room."

"Well, we'll just have to do it over," Jenny said brightly. "Oh, I defrosted your refrigerator for you. We needed ice. I just went ahead and cleaned out the rest of it while I was at it."

"Yeah," Paul interjected, sticking his finger down his throat in a gagging fashion. "I hope you weren't too attached to that alien fetus growing in the orange bowl. I buried it out by the fence. It was a nice service. You would have been proud. Mom said one of her loooong prayers."

"Paul," his mother cautioned, "stop with the nonsense and quit aggravating your sister. Now, let's eat. I'm dangerous when I'm hungry."

"Wait." Paul put his hand up to stop the conversation. "Let's back up to the 'friend'."

Kara gave him a disgusted look. "Here it comes."

"Could this be the 'friend' Jack said has been sniffing around. Kara you know better than to—"

Jenny's mouth pursed. "Sniffing around? Paul, don't be vulgar!" She let her breath out in a huff. "We know nothing about this 'friend' so don't be judgmental."

Paul nodded. "Sorry. Jack did say he was a pretty good guy. He liked working out with him, but he said he had a different girl every time they double-dated." He looked at Kara who was trying to avoid eye contact and continued looking at the ceiling. "Sis, even under normal circumstances, you don't need a womanizer."

Kara slapped her hand on the table. "That's it! His name is Kevin. He's just a friend. He's a lawyer and is helping with the license contract for Kids Haven. What he does in his personal life is no business of mine, yours, OR Jack's. Understood?"

"Woah! Sister's got her dander up. Excuuuuse me."

Jenny butted in, "Okay, you're excused. Now say Grace and

let's eat before it gets too cold."

"Yes, Captain." Paul saluted her. "I doubt if anything can get too cold in this house." He turned to Kara. "You ever going to get air conditioning?"

She grabbed his shoulders and turned him toward the table of food. "Shut your mouth and eat."

"Hmmm, shut my mouth and eat. That would be tricky."

That made Kara laugh. "Mom, are you sure he wasn't adopted?"

They all laughed, sat down, said Grace before devouring the delicious food. They talked about old times, new times and what each had been up to since they helped Kara move to the farm.

"Oh, before I forget," Kara interjected, "Barb was so excited about your visit, she's invited us to a barbeque tomorrow evening at their new house."

Mrs. Peters was visibly excited about seeing Barb again and getting to meet her husband. "I still can't get used to the idea Barb is married," she commented wistfully. "Why it seems only yesterday when she brought you home from first grade that day you got lost."

"Kara never could find her way out of a paper bag," Paul stated.

Kara jabbed him with her fork. "I was only six and we had just moved to that neighborhood, creep!"

"Yes," her mother went on to explain to Paul, "she turned one block too soon. Barb lived across the street from us and had seen us move in so she told Kara how to get home."

"I'm going to have to scold Barb about that," Paul said seriously. "Think how nice life would have been with just us boys."

Kara threatened him with her fork again and he took it away from her through a playful, giggling scuffle and tossed it in the sink.

Their mother shook her finger at them. "You kids cut out the rough-housing and help clean these dishes up. I'm going out to the car and get our things."

"I'll get our things," Paul insisted. "You sit yourself down and relax, while Kara cleans up the dishes."

"Thanks," Kara returned blandly.

"I'm all heart."

"And a lot 'mouth'," she called out as he walked toward his truck.

CHAPTER TWENTY TWO

That night after Paul was snug as a bug on a pallet on the living room floor, Kara turned down the spread on the other twin bed in her room for her mother.

"Your Aunt Edith said to give you her love," the older woman said wearily as she nestled under the sheet.

"How's she doing?" Kara asked, switching off the light.

"Well as can be expected. Mrs. Hargis is looking after her while I'm here."

"Mrs. Hargis is good at nursing," Kara commented remembering their nice neighbor who was always putting calamine lotion on neighborhood children's bug bites almost before the bug had bitten.

"I don't think it's Edith you want to talk about," her mother guessed. "Something's troubling you...I can tell. Is it your job?"

Kara chuckled at her mother's intuition. "That and...well, remember the 'friend' I mentioned the last time we talked on the phone?"

"The friend you were not going to see anymore? But the same friend who helped you with the wall paper?"

"Yes, him. Well...I still think more of him than I should."

"I suspected as much from when we talked before," Jenny returned knowingly. "Is he a nice man? Has Jesus come into his life? You said he was a lawyer. Is he a good one? Is he fair in his dealings? Does he come from a nice family?"

Kara laughed inwardly. If Kevin thought SHE was an interrogator, what would he think of her mother? "To answer you...yes he's nice, Jesus is not a part of his life...yet, yes he's fair, his family is deceased, but I'm sure they were 'nice', but that's sort of a moot point. We have agreed...well, to keep our relationship all business."

"Whose idea was that?"

"Mostly his."

"Oh," Jenny whispered quietly. "Well, we'll just have to see what we can do about that. AND, you know, God has long arms. He'll reach out to Kevin and bring him into—"

"No, Mom, don't you do anything 'about' it. It's just that I needed to talk...to sort it all out."

"I never told Paul about our conversation the last time we talked. So the first Paul heard about your 'friend' was through Jack."

"Well, that 'business arrangement' didn't work out, but we do agree not to be alone together."

"And how's that working for you?"

"Personally, I miss the fun we have together but we haven't seen each other recently."

"How long have you known him?"

"I met him at Barb's wedding."

Jenny shot upright and stared at Kara through moonlit shadows. "Just a few weeks! You fell for him in a couple weeks?"

"No," Kara said calmly and deliberately. "I fell for him in one minute. I think I knew the instant I laid eyes on him. Besides," she also sat up and turned the lamp back on, looking her mother in the eye, "you met daddy one week and *married* him the next."

"That was different. He was leaving for the Army." Jenny turned her back on Kara. "I don't believe I owe you an explanation. Do as I say not as I do."

Kara smiled at her mother's 'gruffness'. "Well, don't worry about it, Mom. It's not like I'm running off to get married like you did. I'm surprised he would even want to be friends with me. He goes more for sophisticated women who live in high-rise apartments and want no more from him than a night out, no commitments, no…" Her voice drifted as she reached up and flipped the light off.

The two women lay in dark silence for a long moment, then Jenny asked quietly. "Are you SURE he's right for you to even be friends with? I can't picture you being attracted to someone as shallow as that."

"Oh, he isn't shallow, Mom. He's had great disappointments in life. He's lost just about everyone he ever loved." She went on to explain the tragic events about Kevin's family and his refusal to love again, and turning from God, ending with, "To answer your first question, yes, I'm sure he would be right for me if I could have a normal life."

"Well, dear, we've always tried to make sure you led a 'normal' life. As concerned as we all were about your illness, we let you do anything you were capable of—even falling in love if that ever happened."

"I know, Mom, and I love you for that, but falling in love would be folly. It would not be fair to him."

Her mother yawned. "Let's sleep on it. Things have a way of working out. I wish there was some way to guide him toward the Lord to help him work through his grief. But about your job. You could change professions. I always felt you were much too tender hearted to be a Case Worker. You're more suited for a career where you can do hands-on type of nurturing."

Kara turned on her side and fitfully punched her pillow. "Mom, I have brought up that subject about God and he's not interested in hearing it."

"Mmmm, time passes, minds change." Jenny's breathing became steadier and heavier with sleepiness. "Like I told you…God has ways to…" Jenny's voice went into an instant snore.

Kara never failed to marvel at her mother's ability to fall asleep so easily. It certainly *was* like 'old times' listening to her mother fall asleep in the middle of her own sentence; and suddenly, Kara felt a sense of well-being wash over her as she, too, drifted into slumber.

****

The next day was spent on outside house repairs that Kara had been unable to do by herself. Paul, as an early birthday present to her, bought enough paint to give the old house a new coat of pale green with dark green trim. She did not know exactly how he did it, but Paul even persuaded Jack to come over and help. They all worked like beavers, with Aaron helping to keep the paint stirred for them, finishing just in time to ready themselves for the barbecue.

Jack left as soon as he cleaned the paint off his hands so he could rest up for the 'hot date' he had that night. The others, though worn to a frazzle and hungry as bears, looked forward to a nice relaxing picnic.

Even though Barb had insisted 'don't bring a thing', Kara's mother made a pan of her famous rhubarb crunch Barb had been fond of as a child and a pot of baked beans. Since Kara had not had time for any 'specialty', her contribution was a couple packages of rolls and Paul's was a case of soda.

The smell of ribs on the grill assailed their nostrils upon arrival, making their mouths water.

"This must be 'da' place," Paul joked, sniffing the air as he gave Barb a friendly hello hug. "How 'ya' been, brat," he asked, calling her by the name he tagged her with many years ago.

"Paul," Barb chided lightly, "if I wasn't so glad to see you, I'd kick you in the shins like I used to when you called me that, but," she added chuckling, "I've got someone to do it for me. John I'd like you to meet 'brother' Paul. Paul, my new husband John Christian who's not only big and tall, but owns a large gun collection."

"Uh, oh," Paul said in mock wariness, holding his hand out in greeting, "guess I'd better be on my best behavior."

They all laughed, kissed and hugged each other for another few minutes before a woman dressed in a strapless apricot-colored sundress and high heeled, backless sandals tippy-toed onto the patio, carrying a molded Jell-O salad that exactly matched the color of her dress.

Gee whiz, Kara mused laughingly, thank heavens my brown and serve rolls match my beige shorts and T-shirt or I would feel utterly, utterly tacky in my blue sneakers.

"Oh," the woman cooed, "your other guests have arrived.

How lovely," she added, smiling without causing a wrinkle in her face while her long coral manicured nails fiddled with the diamond pendant around her neck.

"Oh, Myra," Barb apologized, "I don't believe you know these people. This is my best friend, Kara, her brother Paul and," she leaned over and gave Jenny another peck on the cheek, "this lady is Kara's mom, Jenny, but I claim her too."

"My pleasure," Myra returned politely.

From her tone of voice, Kara half expected her to curtsy and was rather disappointed when she didn't.

"Myra is a friend of a friend of John's." Barb went on to explain while Kara nodded a smiling 'how nice' greeting to the apricot stranger. "Kevin Michals. You know Kevin, don't you, Kara?"

Kara's smile faded to a lopsided grin and froze in place. "Yes," she answered, her voice sounding very distant. "Kevin...yes, I know him."

"I didn't know if I was going to get to come or not," Myra said with a vague hint of disappointment, raking her nails up the side of her platinum hair to put an errant tendril back in the bun on top of her head. "Mother just got out of the hospital."

"Appendix?" Kara asked dazedly.

Myra's perfectly plucked brows raised in surprise. "Why, yes. How did you know?"

"Lucky guess," Kara answered flatly. She felt like the final nail had just been put in her coffin, having met the 'date' Kevin was waiting to jump in the hot tub with that night at Barb's house.

"Kevin is going to be *so* surprised," John related. "He doesn't know Myra's going to be here."

"He...he's coming here?" Kara choked out. "Now? Tonight?"

Jenny took Kara's hand and patted it, feigning sudden thirst to help her daughter out of a sticky predicament. "Sweetheart, why don't you get your poor old parched mother something cold to drink?"

Kara found her way blindly into the kitchen to extract some ice from the refrigerator. She felt every emotion in the books but mostly sick. Kevin was coming here tonight and his date was a piece of orange-colored fluff?

Barb followed her into the kitchen. "You okay? You look weak."

"I'm fine. It's just I didn't expect Kevin to be here."

Barb looked at Kara apologetically. "Sorry about that. John invited him and knew he knew Myra so invited her too. I never told him about you and Kevin."

"Well, there's really nothing to tell."

"Really?"

Kara cocked her head sideways. "Yes, really."

Barb smiled wryly. "Okay, then, could you tell me how the pink robe I bought you for Christmas ended up hanging on the back of the guest bathroom door?"

Kara breathed in and out, then shrugged her shoulders. "I *could* tell you but it wouldn't be as interesting as what you are thinking."

"I'm not 'thinking' what you think I'm thinking...knowing you. I'm just curious. Be sure to take it back home with you or, better yet, I'll bring it to the office. I don't want anyone seeing you carrying it to your car." She raised her brow. "You know...too many unanswered questions."

Kara smiled and gave her friend a hug. "Do me a favor. Don't tell Kevin you found the pink robe."

"Mmmm, like I said...too many unanswered questions. Promise me you'll tell me all about it someday."

"Someday. Now I'd better get this cold drink out to Mom."

"Hey, sis, what happened to ya?" Paul said, coming up behind her.

"I...I...I'm not feeling too well," she lied.

He put his arm around her and led her out through the patio doors. "Poor angel," he soothed genuinely sympathetic. "Too much painting in the heat. Tomorrow you rest...I'll work."

She felt like a heel. While all her brothers were quick to tease and aggravate her, they were just as quick to respond with kindness and concern when she was ill.

"Really, Paul, it's nothing to worry about. I'll be fine."

Her words hung in space when she saw Kevin approaching the party, his eyes instantly showing surprise when he saw her, then turning cold as she watched him eye Paul up and down standing beside her with his arm draped around her waist and planting a big kiss on her cheek.

Kara thought it best to save further embarrassment. She went over to Kevin, before the others were even aware he had arrived, to explain to him that she had nothing to do with this. She did not know he and Myra were invited and certainly didn't want to cause him any further anguish.

"Kevin! I didn't know you would be here."

"I guessed that." He nodded toward Paul.

"Wha...what?" She was clearly puzzled.

"Him?"

"Him who?"

"The blond Mr. America you were snuggled up with on the patio."

Kara glared at him. "You think he's—"

"If you'll excuse me I see someone I haven't seen in a long time." He gave Myra a smile and a two-fingered wave.

"Oh, yes," Kara smirked, also waving affectedly to Myra, "Florence Nightingale tore herself away from her sick mother to be with you tonight. Mustn't keep her waiting."

"I shan't," he stated just as affectedly, hurrying to Myra's side.

So that's the game he wants to play, she fumed. Well, let him think what he wants about Paul. She stomped heatedly back to Paul's side and linked her arm with his as introductions were once more being made by Barb.

"Let's see now, Kevin, I've introduced you to Kara's mother and I believe you already know Kara." He nodded giving Paul the once over again as Barb continued. "That just leaves her br—"

"Paulie," Kara cut in, beaming up at her brother who was frowning at her stupid giddy expression. "This is Paulie."

"Glad to meet'cha, Kevin." Paul thrust his hand forward but was met with a rather limp brush off.

"Yeah, me too," Kevin returned flatly.

"Everybody fill your plates," John called from the grill. "If you go away hungry, it's your own fault."

Most didn't have to be called twice to the food line, but Kara was only going through the motions. Her appetite had been ruined.

"Eating a little heavy tonight, aren't you?" Kevin asked her at the table when she absent-mindedly plopped the third big spoonful of potato salad on the plate.

Realizing what she had done, she quickly lied. "Oh, my, this isn't for me," she lilted, calling, "Paulie, how many of my delicious 'buns' would you like?"

Kevin's eyes narrowed at her 'buns' insinuation. "Speaking of 'buns'," he retaliated, "I wonder what else Myra would like me to put on her plate."

"Oh, give her some beans," Kara huffed, plummeting a scoopful into his plate, "and some lettuce." She heaved a big helping of the greens onto the already overflowing vessel, causing some to drop to the ground.

"Kara, quit it," Kevin cautioned in a loud whisper, wiping bits of baked beans off his shirt.

"And don't forget the apricot Jell-O salad," she continued with diligence, slinging a glob of the soft substance in the middle of the whole mess. "We certainly want Myra to be the same color on the inside as she is on the out."

Just at that moment Myra stepped forth to claim her plate, her lip curling upward. "Kev, darling," she hesitated sickly, "I don't think I can eat all this food." She handed the plate back to him.

"Oh, what a pity," Kara butted in with mock concern, "after 'Kev' went to all that trouble."

"Well…" Myra studied the plate once again, tittering. "I always say if I don't watch my figure, who will?"

Kara tittered back.

"But then, it *was* awfully nice of you, Kev," Myra continued.

"Awfully," Kara mocked.

"Oh, what the heck. A pound or two won't hurt me." Myra reached for the plate.

Kevin pulled it back. "I'll fix you another," he offered politely.

"She said she'd eat it, 'Kev'," Kara ground out over-politely, taking hold of the plate and giving it a yank.

With his thumb in the slick potato salad, Kevin was not able to hold onto it and it sailed like a missile, making a perfect landing on the shelf of Myra's very generous bosom. All mouths gaped as Myra bent over, screeched and dug apricot Jell-O out of her cleavage.

Barb ran to her with paper towels and Kara apologized profusely as she picked lettuce and beans off Myra's bare shoulders. "I can't tell you how sorry I am. Please, let me—"

"Don't touch me," Myra cautioned, backing away from the crowd around her. "Don't anyone touch me." She quickly disappeared into the house.

John found it all rather amusing and had to cover his mouth to keep from laughing, but Kara had never felt so foolish in all her life. She had never felt jealous before and didn't know it made an idiot out of her. She wished she could jump up and kick herself in the rear with both feet. *God, please help me!*

She looked at her mother pleadingly. "I want to go home. I suddenly have a splitting headache."

"And deservedly so," her mother chastised. "Come Paul, we're leaving."

"You haven't eaten," Barb said disappointedly.

"Stay," John suggested to Mrs. Peters. "We'll see that you get home."

"Well," Kara's mother returned, "I *would* like to stay a little longer."

"Good, then that's settled," Barb agreed, giving Kara a friendly, understanding squeeze. "Hope you get to feeling better."

"Thanks. I'm sure I will." Kara returned the hug, her eyes filling with tears of regret for all the commotion she caused. "Please tell Myra again how sorry I am."

She caught sight of Kevin out the corner of her eye as she turned to leave. His hands were jammed into the pockets of his powder blue cotton pants and dots of red bean stain peppered the front. This was her life she was messing up. What had her mother said? Things have a way of working out...minds change...paths cross. Ha! Paths crossed all right, but there was big doubt minds changed.

"Goodbye, everybody," she choked out, waving over her shoulder.

"Kara, wait!"

She faltered a second hearing Kevin's voice, but continued on. There was nothing she could say to him.

He caught up with her just as she got into her car and leaned in the window and grabbed the keys from the ignition.

"I want to talk to you," he insisted.

"There's nothing to talk about...except I'm sorry for making such a scene." She tried to retrieve her keys.

He jerked his hand out of reach. "This is crazy. Every time we get together, the stupidest things happen."

"You're right," she wholeheartedly agreed. "So the best thing is for us not to get together. You've made that perfectly clear so go on back to Myra."

"Kara, I'm not 'with' Myra."

Kara raised her brows. "What do you mean?"

"I don't know what you did to me, but I'm not myself. I can't even cuss anymore."

She laughed. "I can understand you not wanting to see me anymore because I'm a blithering idiot, but not being able to use swear words is about as lame an excuse as I have ever heard."

"That's not why we shouldn't be together and you know it."

"What then?"

"I'm trying to abide by your wishes not to get involved. I'm actually starting to miss your pets. I've missed your neighbor boy. By the way I have a new bike on order for him. Also, about the contract...I negotiated some things in your favor. I'll get it to you."

"Thanks. But go on...you miss my pets? You miss Aaron? You can't cuss? Anything else?"

He reached in the window and placed his finger on her cheek. "I miss you and all the craziness that goes with you, but the most astonishing thing is, I'm beginning to like Old Betsy. If it wasn't for your old car, I would have never gotten acquainted with you."

"That might be a good thing."

"I don't know about that."

"I do. Kevin, God puts us where we need to be and I need to be taking care of Kids Haven and getting it up and running. It's my calling and I know it. I don't want to burden anyone else with it."

He straightened and paced a few steps, then turned to her again. "I don't know why, but I feel responsible for you somehow."

"Look at me. I'm an idiot. I ruined Myra's dress over some snit I was having."

"I'll ask her to send you the cleaning bill if that would help."

"It does not. I need to go home and have a long talk with God. I've certainly not acted in a well-behaved manner lately. He's probably shaking his head about now and wondering what ever happened to the real Kara Peters."

"God's not shaking his head. You are the nicest, kindest person I know."

"Oh, Kevin, think about it. I stripped down to my underwear in front of you."

"That was just one crazy night and nothing really bad happened. I'm sure your God would forgive you for that one indiscretion."

"One?"

"Don't try to tell me my kissing you is classified as an indiscretion. I'll never believe that." He shook his head. "Besides I always thought kissing was a team sport." He chuckled. "I'll not take all the blame for kissing."

"I've got to go, Kevin. Give me my keys."

"Not until I know you're okay."

"Go back to the party...to Myra."

"I told you I'm not with Myra." He let his breath out and glanced down at her. "That's another thing besides not being able to cuss. I've not dated anyone since I met you. Don't even want to."

"Well, I'm sorry for all the changes you think I've made in your life. Maybe Myra can change your mind." She turned her head away from looking at him. "I have a lot of soul searching to do and I can't do it sitting out here arguing with you."

"You jealous?"

"*No!* I am not jealous." She leaned her head on the steering wheel and muttered, "Maybe a little."

"Well, I am 'maybe' a lot jealous."

"Give me a break."

"No, I'm serious. I see that Paulie guy kissing you and I don't know what to think."

"So you thought the worst. You think I'm a tease."

"I don't think that. I just don't want anyone to take advantage of you. You're special. You're different."

"I'm different all right."

"That doesn't make you wrong."

"It makes me wrong for you," she added sadly, lifting her eyes to meet his troubled ones. "Even if I didn't have health problems."

"No," he said quietly. "You're not wrong for me. I'm not right for you. You deserve more than I can give you. Maybe Paulie is the one for you."

"He doesn't like to be called Paulie. He prefers Paul and he's my brother."

She grabbed the keys out of his hand and started the engine. Instantly, the car radio blasted its own Elvis tribute. "YOU AIN'T NOTHIN' BUT A HOUND DOG" blared out over the airwaves.

Kevin plugged his ears and yelled, "Turn it off!"

"The switch is broken," Kara yelled back, slapping at the strategic spot on the dash to get the radio to turn off. It only increased the volume. "I guess Betsy has her own opinion of you."

Kevin shouted as loud as he could. "Why didn't you tell me Paul was your brother?"

"I started to," she cried out above the noise, "but you were too busy 'tootle-looing' Myra." She gave him a disgruntled look and mocked his two-fingered wave as she circled the drive. As one last insult, Betsy backfired and shot an unsightly sooty substance down one leg of Kevin's pants.

Elvis could be heard singing loud and clear…"YOU AIN'T NEVER CAUGHT A RABBIT AND YOU AIN'T NO FRIEND OF MINE."

CHAPTER TWENTY THREE

Kara spent the rest of the evening on the back porch agonizing to her pets about her inadequacies.

"I know you think I'm perfect just the way I am, but I'm very stupid when I'm with Kevin. I had a jealous fit that was shameful."

The pets showed their admiration by sitting as close to her as they could without smothering her.

"To be honest, we both said a lot of things in anger...you know, that jealous thing," she told Pooch referring to her earlier conversation with Kevin.

"I wish I could do today over again. I would have not dumped that plate of food all over Myra...well, maybe I would have, I don't know. That jealous thing just consumed me." She sighed. "I'm going to hate the reprimand I'm going to get from Mom and Paul." She patted the dogs on the head. "Do you think God can forgive me?"

Just then the sound of a car motor interrupted her musings and she rose and peered around the corner of the house, catching sight of Kevin's car pulling into the drive. She jumped back into the darkness out of sight and listened to her mother and Paul laughing hysterically.

"Mom, you are definitely going to have to go on a diet if you're ever going to ride on my lap again?" Paul cajoled.

Holy cow, Kara surmised, they all three crammed into that

little car! She listened again intently as her mother thanked Kevin for the lift home, telling him how delighted she was to have met him. Kara winced when she heard her mother say, "Come go to church with us in the morning."

"Uh, thanks, Mrs. Peters, but I...I have some things I have to do."

"Like what? And call me Jenny," she persisted.

"Like..." He laughed. It was a soft, deep laugh that Kara had heard so many times before, the sound of it causing a rippling surge down her spine. "Things...I can't think of them right now...uh...Jenny," he confessed, embarrassed by his stammering.

"Fine. Then we'll see you here about, oh say, eight thirty. You'll love my blueberry muffins."

"Really, Mrs., I mean Jenny—"

"Eight thirty," she called over her shoulder, walking toward the house. "Don't be late. You'll miss out on the muffins."

Paul laughed. "No point in arguing, Kevin. You won't win."

Kara threw her hands up in exasperation at her mother's insistence. She could clearly see Kevin was trying to get out of going to church in as nice a way as he could, but he just didn't know her mother. She turned and ran into the house, jumped into bed and pretended to be asleep.

Jenny tiptoed into the bedroom, shed her clothing and slipped on her nightgown. "Did I wake you?"

"It's okay. I'll go back to sleep."

"I think you'd rest better if you took your clothes off and put your nightie on."

"Okay, Mom," Kara said getting out of bed, "you caught me. I heard you come home and your conversation with Kevin. Mom, he isn't into church—"

"We'll see."

"We'll see? That's it? You're not going to tell me what an imbecile I was today?"

"Mmmmm," her mother breathed sleepily, "knowing you, you've already said enough to yourself. Now go to sleep. Sweet dreams."

Yes, sweet dreams. If only, Kara thought.

****

Kevin arrived at precisely eight thirty Sunday morning. Kara lingered in the bedroom getting dressed. She was still embarrassed to face him after the fiasco yesterday, but she could hear him greet her mother and Paul as they laughed again about the ride home in his little car.

"Kara's still primping," Paul said as he poured each of them a cup of coffee and set a warm muffin in front of each place setting. "Come on, Sis, get 'em while they're hot," he called out.

Jenny motioned for the boys to go ahead and eat. "She'll be out in a minute." She turned to Kevin. "So, Kara says you've had some heartaches in your life."

Kevin nearly choked on his bite of muffin.

"Oh, don't be embarrassed," Jenny soothed, patting his hand. "We've all had our share of dreadful things. Kara's heart trouble, for instance."

Kevin let his breath out. "I don't know how you all handle that. Kara seems so well adjusted to it. It's just hard to fathom."

"My dear boy, being happy doesn't mean everything in life is a bed of roses. It means you look beyond the bad stuff and be grateful for all the good we have in life." She patted his hand again. "Trust in the Lord. He'll make everything right."

Kevin smiled at her. "I admire what you believe, Jenny. I really do. It…it's just not for me."

"Well, maybe not right now. Maybe you're not ready." She put her cup to her mouth and drained it. "Paul, pour us another cup of coffee."

"Yes, Captain."

"Stop that. I'm trying to have a serious conversation with Kevin."

Paul raised his brows to Kevin and shrugged his shoulders. Kevin nodded letting him know it was okay.

"When you're ready, you'll know. You'll feel like some big airplane swooped down and swept you up to higher ground and left that old Satan trembling in the dust."

"Well," Kevin said smiling, "there's one thing I *do* know. These muffins ARE the very best I've ever eaten."

Kara emerged from the bedroom, dressed in her Sunday

best, smiled and nodded a greeting to Kevin. "Mom, that's enough serious talk. Let's just enjoy your delicious muffins."

Jenny shrugged and shook her head. "I've really only just begun."

"We know, Mom," Paul said, getting Kara a cup of coffee. "Just give it a rest for a while." He then turned to Kevin. "Believe me, you don't need to be concerned with Satan when Jenny Peters is around. He's scared to death of her."

They all laughed loudly—except for Jenny.

****

Sunday passed with mixed emotions. Kara and Kevin's relationship wasn't quite as strained as Kara had thought it might be, but neither was it the joyous one she might have hoped for.

Despite her mother's 'preaching', Kevin was very relaxed around her and commented several times how wonderful it must be to have a large family sharing the love they had for one another. He confessed it made him think of his own family he once had, but Kara could see the pain on his face when he was reminded of the hurt he suffered losing them.

Her heart reached out to him and she wanted so much to get through to him how God's Grace could see him though anything. She couldn't deny her strong feelings for him and wanted to pray his hurt away.

"Kevin," she said, putting her hand on his shoulder, "thanks for today. It made mom very happy. Me too."

"Me too," he repeated. "Your mom is wonderful. Paul too. He's the kind of brother every sister should have."

"Well, thanks. I agree," she returned with a smile.

Jenny walked up to them. "How about lunch? I feel like eating myself into a coma before we go back to Kara's and tackle some more renovations."

"Works for me," Paul said, taking his mother by the arm. "Come on, old gal, I'll escort you to Betsy."

"Old gal!" Jenny jerked her arm away from him. "I'll 'old gal' you. You're not too big for a spanking."

"She's right. She gets dangerous when she's hungry. Her sense of humor goes by the wayside," Paul chided.

Old Betsy never wavered during their trip into downtown Peoria, and the radio stayed silent which surprised everyone. After a huge lunch including dessert, they waddled back to the car moaning about eating too much.

Jenny chuckled. "When I go to an all-you-can-eat buffet, I feel obligated to do just that. I'm miserable but it was worth it."

When they arrived at the farm, Kevin excused himself and said he needed to go home. "It's been a pleasure." He took Jenny into his embrace and hugged her for a long time.

"The pleasure was mine," she returned softly.

He then shook Paul's hand, turned and smiled at Kara. "See you in court."

She smiled back weakly as he got in his car and left.

After a short rest, her mom, Paul and she sprang into action on repairs and fix-ups. Kara was so grateful for their help and profusely expressed her love for them. "You guys outdid yourselves. Mom, I hope you're not too worn out."

"Me? I don't get worn out. You know that. But I need you to promise *me*, you won't get too worn out. You look tired and stressed."

"I'm fine, Mom," she tried to assure, even though she knew she had not been feeling perky lately. She attributed it to worrying about Teresa Becker, and her feelings for Kevin, both of which did make her feel a little weary at times.

After a tearful goodbye to her mother and brother on Monday afternoon, Kara sat down and prayed. *Why? Why God? Why would you bring someone into my life when you know I could not fulfill his life? I have, through Your help, come to terms with the fact I may not live much longer. You have given me many wonderful years beyond anyone's expectations and I am so grateful. Grateful beyond belief.*

She decided she would change everything. For the short time she may have left, she needed to concentrate on what her goal has been. Kids Haven. It was ready to open and she would be needed to help run it. Barb would be devastated, but Kara decided the best thing would be to give her notice, but agree to stay until a suitable replacement could be found.

Leaving her job would put a real strain on her finances, so the only thing she had that was worth anything, was…she choked back a sob…Old Betsy.

Paul and her mother had helped her make tremendous headway with the house, laying the kitchen tile and the rest of the painting and papering. The house now looked presentable enough for a king, she thought. There was only one thing left on her list, and that one thing was the hardest decision she had to make.

She walked out to Old Betsy and got in behind the wheel, her eyes welling with tears. "I know we've been together for a long, long time, but you understand, don't you, old girl?" She poked fondly at the rip in the upholstery. "I love you, but look at it this way, maybe someone will buy you who can afford new paint for you. You'll look so nice." She laughed through her tears. "I probably won't even recognize you if we ever meet on the street."

Glancing up in the rearview mirror, Kara lifted her hair on top of her head and studied her reflection. "Maybe with a new hairdo, chances are you won't recognize me either, old friend." If she could find the courage, she'd call Kevin's mechanic Brad, and see if he could contact the buyer he mentioned. She needed desperately to change her life and try to manage getting her feelings for Kevin under control. A different hairdo, a couple new outfits, something to make her feel good enough about herself to do what needed to be done while she still had the time. *Dear God, give me the courage to do Your will.*

She suddenly felt very empty and drained. It was all she could do to walk back into her house. Her breathing was labored. She quickly retrieved the oxygen tank and put the mask on, holding her cell phone in her hand in case she needed to call for help.

No, God, it's not time yet. I need Your healing hands.

Just before midnight her breathing was normal again and she could feel her pulse beating at a steady beat. She removed the mask and breathed in and out several times to assure she was okay.

Thank you, Lord.

CHAPTER TWENTY FOUR

The next week was like something out of a horrible dream. Her 'transformation' did not make her happy. When she looked in the mirror she didn't see Kara Peters at all. She saw a stranger with hair twisted into a French roll and eye makeup to make her lashes longer. She looked like a well-bred, intelligent individual with sophistication just oozing out all over her, but she didn't feel that way.

She had called Brad about selling Betsy but the buyer was out of town for a few weeks. Brad offered to help her find a sensible compact car when she was ready, that got at least thirty miles to the gallon and the radio turned on and off with the switch. It all sounded so boring.

Of course, she missed Kevin but knew she had to keep her distance in order to 'get over him' as she kept telling herself. The two times she had run into him on the courthouse steps, he had certainly done a double take, questioning her appearance.

"Done something new to your hair?"

"Thought I'd try something different."

"You did. It's different." He looked her up and down again. "Want to have lunch?"

Her heart skipped a beat but she managed a 'sophisticated' check of her appointment app on her cell. "Sorry, too busy."

She watched him shrug and walk away. All those clever things she used to want to say, she was actually saying now. Was she proud of herself? No. She was miserable.

****

Time passed slowly over the next couple of weeks. Barb did not want to accept her resignation and said she would table it until Kara had time to think about it more.

Spending time with Teresa made not spending time with Kevin a little more bearable, but she felt herself getting extremely attached to the girl and it was becoming harder and harder to let a day pass without seeing her.

One particular evening early in the third week of her 'transformation' when she was hurrying to get to Teresa's house, she found Kevin leaning nonchalantly against Old Betsy's door.

"You're a hard lady to get hold of now days," he said in a friendly tone. "I keep getting that answering machine of yours."

"Yes, well, I'm sorry I haven't been able to return your calls. I've been pretty busy."

"I see that." His gaze raked over her from her head to her feet.

She dropped her head to hide the rush of blood that went to her cheeks, caused by his scrutiny.

"Still got your 'different' hairdo, I see."

She raised her head. "Yes." She twiddled with the cross on a chain around her neck. There was a long embarrassing silence, then she finally asked, "Was…was there something you wanted?"

"Yeah," he answered, still studying her with a critical eye. "How does Aaron like his new bike I had delivered?"

"Crazy about it." She smiled broadly and for a second the old Kara seeped through and it felt good. "And on behalf of everyone in a five mile radius, I want to thank you for having it equipped with a horn that would wake the dead."

"My pleasure."

"Well, think pleasure when you get the bill for my hearing aid."

They both laughed. Then it dawned on her she was letting down her guard. She immediately put her features back in 'non-wrinkling' order. "Is that all you needed?"

"Kara, what's wrong? Are you all right?" He was clearly concerned.

"Of course, I'm fine. Why?"

"I'm worried about you…you don't seem yourself."

"Really, Kevin. A girl gets a new hairdo and—"

"It's not just that…it's…" He stopped and studied her. "Are you feeling okay? I talked to Jack and he's worried too."

She breathed in noisily. "If this is some more of your 'brotherly' concern, Kevin, I really must be going. I have an appointment."

"A date?"

"No."

"Then how about dinner?"

"I can't. I have to go, I'll be late."

"Lunch tomorrow?"

She reached into her purse and pulled out her cell, but his large hand closed over hers. His touch ignited every nerve ending she had. It was with a great deal of fortitude she was able to keep breathing normally.

"Just lunch, Kara. Can that cut into your 'busy schedule' all that much?"

Stay cool and calm, she instructed herself. "Well, maybe a quick lunch."

"Thanks. I know your passion for Coney dogs, so I thought—"

"Oh, no," she lied. "I'd much prefer the prime rib at the Continental."

He looked at her questionably, stepping aside and opening the car door for her. "Okay if that's what you want."

She got in and leaned out the window. "I'll meet you there…oh say," she made a strong point to sound casual, "noonish?"

Mild amusement spread over Kevin's face. "Noonish it is."

Kara spent the evening with Teresa, telling her about a children's craft show she wanted to take her to at the mall one afternoon. She reluctantly left Teresa's house just before dark. When the little girl smiled and pointed to Old Betsy, Kara nodded agreement.

"I know. I'm having a hard time making myself sell her."

She breathed wistfully. "Hopefully it will all be worth it in the end."

****

Sleep was unusually difficult that night. Perhaps it was the excitement of having lunch with Kevin or maybe it was the strain of putting up a false front. She felt she was making some headway. There were days when she only thought about him twenty-three hours out of twenty-four. Who was she kidding? She doubted she would ever get him out of her mind.

Finally, lunchtime came and she pulled into the Continental's parking lot, then walked casually into the dining room. Kevin was already there looking so handsome in his dark suit.

"Am I late?" she asked.

Kevin looked at his watch. "Noonish. Right on time."

She surprised herself how reserved she could be around him. Lunch went by without a hitch, their conversation was pleasantly impersonal and Kevin seemed to cling to every 'sophisticated' remark she made about the oil crisis.

When Kevin walked her to her car and his arm brushed against hers, her disguise was nearly blown. It had been so long since she had been that near him, the merest touch made her feel like she had swallowed a lighted sparkler.

"The leaves are starting to turn," Kevin commented. "I'll bet it's beautiful out at your place."

A glorious picture of the fall colors displayed by the trees in her yard came immediately to her mind's view, but she casually flipped, "I really haven't noticed. I've spent so little time there since I finished decorating. I've been very busy with…with civic and cultural activities…"

"You've finished the place?" he asked with interest. "I'd love to see it."

"Mmm, I don't think so. It's just something I did to while away my time." This was even hard for *her* to swallow. She crossed her fingers behind her back, hoping for forgiveness for her shallowness.

"Kids Haven doing okay?"

"Yes," she said honestly. "I want to thank you for the tweaks you made in the contract. If you'd send me your bill…"

"Kara," he interrupted, grabbing hold of her hand. "I've never known you to be so…so uncaring about things. You were always so adamant about fixing up your farm house." His brows knitted. "Who are you?"

"Oh, really Kevin, you worry too much."

He let her hand go. "Maybe so." He looked into her eyes. "Will we be able to see each other again?"

She hung her head, unable to keep up the 'sophisticated' façade. "I don't know. We did agree to stay away from each other."

"Yeah, I know, but…"

They looked at each other and roared very 'unsophisticated' at the familiar phrase. For a brief second Kara felt relieved to just enjoy a very delightful moment with Kevin…something she hadn't done for a long, lonely time.

Still not wanting to appear too eager, Kara accepted Kevin's invitation to dinner the following Saturday. That gave her three days to calm her throbbing heart and study up on some more world problems to discuss during their date. The natural habitats of the tsetse fly might be a good topic.

Yes, tsetse flies. That should sufficiently bore him to the point he would never ask her out again.

CHAPTER TWENTY FIVE

Kara tried to feel happy about her change in lifestyle, but a strange niggling kept poking at her conscience. She felt she was back-sliding from God. Could she ever be forgiven for living this way? It was almost as bad as her mother preaching, 'like yourself and others will like you'. She laughed. Just like Mom. She can be miles away but she sends her spirit down to nag.

She had to do something to change things. She needed to go on with her goal and let Kevin get back to his life. As long as they kept seeing each other, it was getting harder and harder not to stay sensible. But she did consent to having dinner with him, so she'd make the best of it.

Getting ready for a date took much longer these days. There was the elaborate hairdo and extra time to apply eye shadow and mascara. Also, her time was cut several minutes to allow her to get to the restaurant by seven thirty. Kevin had wanted to drive out to pick her up, but in keeping with her 'new image' she insisted on picking him up.

"Okay, how do I look?" she asked the pets, twirling around on the porch to show off the pale green silk dress with matching shawl.

Smokey and Scooter didn't even look up and Pooch only gave one feeble flop of his tail.

"That bad, huh? Don't blame you. I don't like me either."

Fortunately, Kevin was more appreciative of her attire and

complimented her several times on her appearance, never failing to touch her hand in the process. It wasn't that she didn't love his touch, it was just that it played havoc with her senses and she was barely able to concentrate on the food, let alone talk about tsetse flies.

Finally after a long silence, Kevin said, "When we get back to my apartment, would you like to come in and see my new divan?"

She hesitated, then answered, "Is that anything like, do you want to see my 'etchings'?"

A flash of humor crossed his face. "More like leather. You do like leather don't you?"

"Of course...leather...I LOVE leather." She snapped her fingers in the air. "Check please!" She motioned for the waiter with one hand which was caught in midair.

"*If* you don't mind," Kevin scolded, putting her hand back on the table. "I may have gone along with your crazy idea about picking me up, but I'll be struck dead if I'll let you pay for the meal."

She acquiesced and obediently allowed him to have his way. Then he took her arm and escorted her to the parking lot.

"Would you like to drive Old Betsy?" she asked politely.

"Me?" He gave the car a once over inspection. "She won't squirt oil on me or something, will she?"

With Kevin behind the wheel and listening to an Elvis tune, they soon arrived at his apartment. "She's pretty comfortable. Kind of like sitting on my couch while driving. Nice," Kevin complimented.

"I told you she's a jewel."

"You know," he said later as they entered the elevator of his apartment building, "there's something strange going on. We've been together twice this week and nothing weird has happened. Even Betsy cooperated. Didn't die, didn't even play the radio too loud. Trouble used to follow us, but now..."

"Gee, maybe I should throw down a banana peel for you to slip on," she suggested dryly. "This is what you wanted, isn't it? A friendship with no surprises?"

"Sure..." He thought a moment. "Of course, who wouldn't? It's just, I don't know, strange. I just wonder whatever happened to that crazy lady who used to live in your body." He laughed. "What is the matter with me? I'm acting like I miss lunacy."

Kara hung her head. "I don't know where that crazy lady went."

The elevator door opened on the top floor and he escorted her into his apartment.

She breathed in. "What is that smell?"

"Automatic air freshener," he said pointing to a small vial plugged into the wall socket. "Like it?"

"Ah, nice." She nodded and cleared her throat nervously, then laughed. "I have automatic dog and cat smells."

"Well that can be nice too…kind of."

She touched the navy blue leather couch, then sat down on it. "This must be the divan in question," she stated glibly, trying to keep her heart still while running her hand along the smooth surface.

The situation was becoming more awkward by the minute. Alone with him in his gorgeous apartment made her skin prickle, but she forced herself to stay aloof. The most difficult problem was pretending she didn't know he was feeling the same uneasiness.

Her eyes raised to meet his and her blood soared to her head, causing dizziness. He had moved closer and his nearness caused an ache in her very core, jangling the stupid 'sophisticated' shell she had built around herself.

"Kara…I…I don't know how to say this." His voice was hoarse as he reached for her.

"Kevin," she cautioned, trying to swallow the lingering lump in her throat. "We can't. "

"I know. That's not what I'm trying to say." His breathing was noisy and labored. "Please don't take this wrong. You're very beautiful with your new hair, new clothes and your eye makeup, but I'd like to have the old Kara back. I miss the fun times we had."

Her emotions overpowered her sensibility and she rose to meet his inviting arms, twining her own around his waist and tilting her face up to meet his descending mouth with hers. Weeks of separation melted into one searing kiss. She craved the intimacy with him she had not felt since becoming the 'new' woman.

She pulled away suddenly, tears streaming down her face. She grabbed a tissue from the side table and swiped at the running mascara. "I hate this stuff," she said looking at the black streaks on the tissue.

"Sweetheart." He reached to pull her back.

"No, can't you see," she sobbed. "I care about you; I can't be 'just friends'. And I certainly can't be this person I've tried to make myself into to help me get you off my mind and me off yours."

"Don't upset yourself."

"No, hear me out." She grabbed another tissue and blew her nose. "You've probably heard people say, 'it's against my religion' when they refuse to do things. Well, everything I've done lately has been against my religion and it is going to stop right now. I want the old Kara back too."

He took her by her shoulders and sat her back down on the couch. "I'm sorry I caused you to be distraught."

"You didn't. I've been down on myself, but God sees me through sorrowful times and He will get me through this. I can't continue to hate myself. Love conquers hate. God wants me to love myself as well as Him and I haven't loved myself lately." She caught her breath. "For every day God has given me here on earth, I will follow His plan for me and I don't expect anyone else to follow that plan with me."

Kevin took her hand. "I've said it before but it's never been so true. You are the bravest, most fearless woman I have ever met. I don't know if I could be as brave as you with what you have to endure."

"I think you could. The devil tries to turn us his way, but faith in Jesus and our God can defeat Satan at every turn. You just have to have undying faith. I know, or at least hope, when I do leave this world, I will be in a beautiful place. I'll see Gramps, my dad and best of all, I'll see Jesus."

"Don't talk about dying."

"It's going to happen."

"Well, I don't think your God could keep you out of heaven with all the good things you have done." Kevin patted her hand.

"Oh, it's not things we do or don't do that will get us to

heaven. It's our relationship with Jesus. We can do all sorts of wonderful things, but unless we have faith in our Lord..."

"Can we change the subject? This is too much stress on you. You look pale."

"I'm fine." She chuckled. "It's because I've wiped off all my makeup."

"You're still beautiful to me." He settled back on the divan. "I can't be 'just friends' either, but I don't want to cause you any more distress than I already have."

"Oh, Kevin, you haven't caused me distress. I've caused myself distress, trying to be someone I'm not." Her voice lowered sadly. "I understand why it is foolish for us to fall in love with each other, but I can't help the way I feel. I don't want you to think anything can come of it. I need to be nothing to you."

"You could never be nothing to me." He took her hand and squeezed it. "Let's talk about something pleasant. How's your brother?"

"Irritating."

"Then I take it he's just fine. And your lovely mother?"

"She's great...busy getting ready for her church's annual garage sale."

"I have a crush on your mom. It might have been the blueberry muffins."

Kara laughed. "I think the feeling is mutual. She talks about you a lot when I call. About what a nice man you are, and soooo handsome."

"Mmmm, she thinks I'm handsome? Nice."

"She hopes I've convinced you to trust in the Lord. I told her I think she and I both have said enough on that subject. Faith in Jesus is an individual decision. We can pray you find His grace in your life, but it's up to you."

She turned and gazed into his tortured blue eyes, her voice lowering affectionately. "After I learned the reason why you won't allow yourself to love; losing your beloved family, I think I loved you more. The really sad thing is, Kevin, I have more faith in your ability to be a loving, caring human being than you do yourself. Even if it can't be me you love, I truly want you to have someone in your life. I really do."

They looked at each other for what seemed an eternity before Kevin slowly pulled her into his arms, cradling her head with his hand. She nestled against his chest and breathed in the manly fragrance.

"Kara," he said softly and tenderly, "I wish you could allow things to be different. I have never been so touched by a woman before." He tilted her chin up with one finger and kissed her lips lightly. "I do care very much. I care that I've hurt you. I care that I let this go on long after I knew what was happening. I'm a selfish person, Kara. I wanted to make love to you that night at my apartment and thought very little about the consequences. I *still* want to make love to you, but I would cut my heart out before I'd hurt you anymore." His voice was a husky whisper.

She heard nothing but his breathing in and out, then finally, he said, "I worry about you."

"And I worry about your worrying about me. Jack does enough of that. I need to get back to my old self, and you need to get back to your perfect life where you can cuss and date whomever you want. I don't want you to go through life having to worry about me."

"I can't help it. You mean a lot to me." He chuckled softly. "But the selfish me can't lie. You bring out...uh...manly urges in me."

"We can't..."

"I know." He kissed her on her forehead.

She giggled. "Besides I never really got 'sophisticated' enough to carry a...a..."

"Gun?"

They laughed for a long moment, then decided they had better call it a night, knowing their goodbye was more than just for the moment. As strong as their physical bond was between them, it wasn't meant for them to be together and they both sadly knew it.

CHAPTER TWENTY SIX

Kara's cases mounted over the next few days. She became more and more frustrated by all the hardships she encountered and all the rules and regulations to be dealt with just to place a child in a safe and loving atmosphere. Barb told her she had not found anyone to take her place yet, but Kara suspected she wasn't trying all that hard.

She worried constantly about all the children she tried to help, but mostly it was Teresa who occupied her thoughts. Kara had finally found a special school for her, but no progress had been made. Teresa still refused to speak.

When Kara learned one particular Tuesday the school was closed due to a water leak, she took a day's sick leave. After Wynona Becker left for the rehabilitation center, Kara picked Teresa up and took her home with her. She knew it was against policy, but it was just something she had to do. She shut off both her cell and home phone so they wouldn't be disturbed while they chatted with the animals on the back porch.

Teresa showed so much excitement watching the pets bow their heads in prayer that she kept giving them treats just to watch them show off. Just as Kara was showing Teresa a 'play dead' trick she had taught Scooter, Kevin pulled into the drive, slammed on the brakes and jumped out of the car.

"What in the world…what are you doing?" he yelled, seeing Kara clutching the little girl to her side. "That's Teresa, isn't it?"

"How did you know we were here?"

"Barb called me," he explained heatedly. "She couldn't leave the office. She said you had taken the day off sick, and she had been trying to reach you by phone. Your house phone is out of order or something and your cell goes right to your voice mail. We thought you might be...anyway, she got worried and asked me to see what was wrong. I SEE what's wrong?"

"This is none of your business," Kara snapped back, motioning Teresa to go play with the dogs in the yard. Teresa left her side but squatted down with Pooch nearby, her eyes keeping frightened vigil on Kara.

"I'm making it my business." He lashed out at her. "You can't take children into your home like you do stray animals! What's going to happen when they discover the child is missing? I'll tell you what will happen, your butt's going to be in the sling."

"Kevin, watch your language."

"Kara, listen to what I'm telling you, for crying out loud!" He grabbed her by the shoulders. "If I have to shake some sense in you I will."

"I'm not your concern anymore, remember?" Her eyes filled with tears. The pain was still there. Seeing him again only brought back the misery of their last goodbye.

He pulled her to him. "I'm afraid you'll always be a concern of mine." He smoothed his hand over her shoulder and down her arm.

"Kevin..." Her arms went instinctively around his neck as he claimed her lips in a hungry, searching kiss.

"This doesn't even make sense," Kevin finally said in a troubled voice.

"I know." She stepped back as tears once more welled and overflowed.

"I'm sorry. I don't want to fight with you." He reached for her again, but she moved clear of his touch. It was too painful.

Suddenly they heard a whimpering sound coming from Teresa as the little girl came running to them. She touched the tears on Kara's cheek, then ran to Kevin screaming, "Stop it, stop it!" She pounded on Kevin's leg. "Don't hurt her anymore," she sobbed.

"Teresa, no, I'm all right," Kara told her, cradling the child in her arms.

Stunned at what was happening, Kevin turned his attention to the little girl. "Let me talk to her," he said, squatting down and taking her onto his lap. He rubbed his hand up and down Teresa's arm to soothe her tenseness and kissed her on the cheek. "That's what I was doing to Kara," he explained. "She was crying because..." he looked up at Kara searching for words, "because she was happy to see me," he finished, causing a weak smile to cross Kara's face.

"I was scared," Teresa squeaked out. Her voice was little and sweet and Kara nearly cried again at the wonderful sound of it.

"You never have to be scared of anything again," Kevin assured. "I'll make sure of it." He looked up at Kara who was wiping the tears from her eyes, tears of joy over Teresa speaking. "Kara, I'm sorry I caused such a disturbance. When I saw you weren't sick, I just thought...thought you had, I don't know...kidnapped her or something."

Kara laughed. "Only for the day, and don't be sorry. If things hadn't happened like they did, she might have never spoken." She kneeled beside Kevin holding the girl on his lap and asked, "Teresa, can you tell us what made you stop talking?"

The child shook her head no.

"You don't know or you don't want to say?" Kara questioned.

The child nodded yes.

"You can tell us," Kevin prodded gently.

"He'll hurt my mommy."

"Who'll hurt your mommy?" Kara cut in.

"Daddy. He said if I told on him he'd come back." She broke down and sobbed, her little shoulders shaking. Kevin held her tighter. "He came back, Kara, and hit her. I never told anyone, honest. I never told and he came back anyway."

"Oh, sweetheart." Kara pulled her from Kevin's lap and hugged her, kissing away her tears. "It's not your fault. You didn't do anything wrong."

Finally Kevin rose. "I've got to admire you, Kara. You may be unethical, but you sure know how to handle kids. I don't know how you make it through all the heartbreak, emotionally."

"I don't do so well at that."

"Well, we'd better get her back home and call Barb before the cops start looking for us."

"The cops won't be looking for us. If you had let me explain, I only intended to keep Teresa for the day to let her play with the animals and see if she might respond to them"

He let out a tension relieving sigh, but insisted on driving them to Teresa's house despite Kara's fear of involving him in breaking the code of confidentiality.

"I'm afraid it's a little late for that. I'm already involved," Kevin theorized. "But don't worry, I'll forget I was ever here."

Kara reluctantly agreed to let him drive them, but Teresa insisted they go in Old Betsy. The child even hummed along with the radio, much to Kevin and Kara's delight even though Teresa was humming a totally different tune than Elvis was singing. Kara was elated Teresa could talk again, but was frightened for her now that she knew for sure that 'Tom' obviously visited them now and again. She was still in deep thought about it when they left Teresa in her mother's care.

"I thought you'd be in better spirits by now," Kevin said as he drove her home.

"Oh, I am," she admitted. "That was a big hurdle we got over, giving Teresa her voice back." She put her hand on his arm. "I have you to thank for that."

"Kara, if you're not busy some evening this week, I'd like to spend some time with you...to talk."

She noted his troubled expression. "Okay, I guess."

They stopped in the driveway and got out of the car. Kara walked with him to his car and watched him get in behind the wheel. "Thanks, again, Kevin."

"No problem." He looked up at her. "What evening would be good for you for our talk?"

"Friday's good for me. I could use a friend to talk to."

"What's your problem?"

"We don't know where Teresa's father is, but now we know he shows up periodically, and I feel Teresa is in jeopardy living there."

"Don't tell me you're considering removing her from her

home?"

"I've been wrestling with the pros and cons. She could always come stay at Kids Haven."

"You'd better brush up on the law."

"Laws! I thought back there with Teresa you had found some compassion."

"Hear me out," he stated calmly. "You'll not have a chance in court with this one. The law clearly states that a parent who is addicted to alcohol or who is a drug addict as defined in the Dangerous Drug Abuse Act and—"

"And who has constantly failed to cooperate in a rehabilitation program for a period of at least twelve months is determined to have failed to have met the Minimum Parenting Standards. I know the law forward and backward, Kevin," she blurted, "but that doesn't keep me from being concerned for Teresa."

"Concerned, yes, but take my advice. Don't go before the judge with your emotions. He only deals with facts and the fact is that child's mother is trying to better herself. If you want to do something, have a peace bond put on the father. Then if he shows his rotten face around there—"

"I'm still going to...to see that Teresa is protected."

Kevin reached out and touched her arm. "Whether you want to admit it or not, you're looking for an excuse to try to care for Teresa yourself."

Kara pulled away. "You're crazy. I'm only thinking of the welfare of the child!"

"Who are you trying to convince, me or yourself?"

"Goodnight, Kevin. We will probably never see eye to eye on this subject so let's just drop it." She turned and started to walk away, then turned back. "What was it you wanted to talk to me about?"

"Our emotions are too raw tonight. I'll see you Friday."

She walked toward her house and was greeted by her eager pets, but didn't feel like playing, so she let them come into the house with her. When she heard Kevin drive away a short time later, she laid her head down on the table and cried. Pooch whimpered and rested his head in her lap.

"Thanks, pal." She treated him with a pat. "He's right, you

know. I *am* secretly wanting to take care of Teresa. Mom has told me all along. I'm NOT suited to be a case worker."

After much soul-searching, she prepared a formal letter of resignation stating she would be leaving immediately. She knew it might be a hardship on Barb if she couldn't find a replacement right away, but there was no use in putting it off any longer.

****

"I hate to see you quit so suddenly," Barb said the next day.

Kara smiled at her friend. "Suddenly? I told you weeks ago."

"I know, but it still seems sudden. I know it's been hard on you, but you really have done a lot of good."

"Not really," Kara returned sadly. "For every foot I've gained, I've backslid a mile. Mom said I probably had too much compassion for kids to be in a job like this one. She's right. I could give myself half a lifetime and I still couldn't trust myself to not get emotionally involved in a case again." She looked wistfully out the window. "I stopped by to tell Teresa and her mother I wouldn't be their case worker any longer."

"And?"

"And," Kara repeated with a tone of reluctance, "I think they are going to be just fine, even without me. Wynona said everything had been taken care of. I don't know what she meant but she looked so happy and so did Teresa. That's all that mattered to me."

Barb chuckled. "I'm sure they will be fine." She picked up a folder from her desk. "I may be able to shed some light on the subject. Something came in over the hot line." She turned a few pages in the folder. "Here it is. Yes, Becker." She read over the report. "Mmm, seems like some good Samaritan turned Tom Becker into the authorities. He's in custody right now."

"Custody? What for? How did they find him?" Kara was so elated she could hardly speak. She took the report from Barb's hand. "I don't care if it's for jaywalking, he's in jail. That's all that counts." Her smile turned into puzzlement when she caught sight of Kevin Michals' name on the report. "Look at this, Barb. Does this mean what I think it means?" She handed the report back.

Barb picked up the phone and called the police station to find out the particulars. She was informed that Kevin Michals had watched the Becker house most of the night suspecting Tom Becker would show up. Kevin had been right and informed the police immediately of Becker's whereabouts. They had been looking for him for years, it seemed.

"Thank God, Kevin followed the rules like he always told me to do. He called the police." Kara chuckled. "I would have probably barged in and tried to subdue the man myself."

"Yeah, you would have, silly girl." Barb laughed with her. "Seems Tom Becker was wanted not only in Illinois, but several other states for various felonies. Tom Becker will not be causing any trouble for a long, long time."

Kara's eyes misted. Kevin. He had kept his promise to Teresa. He told her he would make sure she was never scared again.

"So…what are you going to do now?"

"I don't know. Take care of Kids Haven for sure, but maybe get a job I'm more suitable for after I run out of money to live on."

"What about Kevin?"

"What about him?"

"I wish things could have turned out differently for you and him. I really feel you were meant for each other." Barb held her hand up. "I know, I know, you're never going to get involved romantically, but you're both such caring people."

Kara raised her brows. "I got the impression Kevin fights 'caring'." She reminded herself that he did say he cared for her, but it was in a 'worrying' type caring she did not want to burden him with.

Barb leaned forward and whispered, "Don't let that barrier he's built around himself fool you."

"But…"

"No buts," Barb cut in. "He'd kill me for telling this…he is soooo private…but he donated hours of his own time handling the legal aspects of getting the grant for the Senior Citizens Center and then matched the funds received from the government with his own."

Kara moaned. "And I thought he spent his money foolishly, buying women gifts."

"He makes people think that. He's really something else. And as far as women are concerned, Jack told John he can't even get Kevin interested in double dating with him anymore."

"I half wish you hadn't told me."

"Why?"

"It only makes me love him more."

"Did you ever think he might feel the same about you?"

"He worries about me is all."

"So? We all do."

"Well, don't. You have John and your wonderful life. Kevin would have me strapped to his back, worrying himself to death."

"You're so wrong in so many ways, sweetie, but it's your life and I'll butt out...for now." Barb let out a sigh. "I'll sure miss you around here. Please take care of yourself."

"I promise."

"You've not been yourself lately. I hope leaving the stress of this job will perk you up again."

"I'm sure it will." Kara gave her friend one last hug before leaving to go clean out her desk. I pray it will, she said to herself.

CHAPTER TWENTY SEVEN

Friday afternoon Kara's cell phone rang, bringing her out of her reverie.

"Hello." Her voice was barely above a whisper.

"Kara? You okay?"

"Oh, Kevin. Yes, I'm just tired. I'm in the Kids Haven sprucing up the living quarters. The couple from church are moving some more of their belongings in tomorrow and I'm adding a few touches to make it comfy for them."

"Save it. I'll help you when I come this evening."

"Thanks, but I'm actually through. I was just sitting in one of the recliners thinking about the 'after school' program. There're several activities planned and I'm very hopeful we can reach a lot of children to show them the love and attention they deserve."

"I'm sure you will, but I still think you're wearing yourself out. Please let someone help you."

"Did you want something?" she asked, deliberately changing the subject.

"I called your office and Barb said you left...for good. I'm behind you on that decision. That job did a number on you."

"Speaking of 'that job', I want to thank you from the bottom of my heart for what you did for Teresa and her mother."

"Strictly my pleasure. Men like Tom Becker should be incarcerated. I have no use for men who beat up women or abuse children. I'll work until my dying day to get as many as I can off the street."

"You're a good man, Charlie Brown."

"Yeah, yeah, I'm a peach. Another thing, I was talking to Brad and he said you were wanting to sell Betsy. What's that all about?"

"I'm thinking about it. I may need the money when my inheritance from Gramps runs out."

"I really need to have a talk with you before you do anything rash, so how about I bring supper tonight. Coney dogs or pizza. What's your pleasure?"

"Oh, Kevin. I'm really not good company right now. Could we make it next week?"

"No, we can't. You don't have to talk, just listen to what I have to say. So, Coney dogs or pizza."

She sighed. He was not going to take no for an answer. "Coney dogs."

"You got it. I'll bring a couple plain hotdogs for the pets. See you around seven."

Kara leaned her head back on the recliner, wondering what in the world Kevin wanted to talk to her about face to face that he couldn't say over the phone. She sighed again and closed her eyes. Maybe all she needed was a nap.

****

Kevin arrived at the farm a little before seven, supper in hand, when Pooch came running out to him emitting a pitiful whining howl. The dog made a circle around him, then ran back to the porch, then back to Kevin.

"What is it, Pooch? You smell hotdogs?"

Pooch let out a loud yelp and ran back to the porch.

Kevin's heart jumped to his throat. Something was definitely wrong. He ran as fast as his legs would carry him, up the porch steps and through the back door to find Kara lying on the kitchen floor, gasping for breath.

"Kara!" He knelt down and cradled her in his arms. "What's happening? What can I do?"

"Ca...can't bre...breathe." She feebly raised her arm to

point toward the oxygen tank.

Kevin gently laid her back down and brought the tank to her. He knew enough to put the mask over her nose and was able to figure out how to get the oxygen flowing to her, but she wasn't responding as quickly as he thought.

"I'd better call for an ambulance."

"No...no time."

He quickly jumped up, dumped the contents of his supper sack into the dogs' bowls, then found her car keys.

"I'll carry you to Betsy so you can lie down in the back seat. Can you hang on without the mask for a few minutes? I'll come back for it after I get you settled in the seat."

She nodded, then closed her eyes.

He scooped her up into his arms and hurried to the car. "Stay with me, babe. Can you hear me?" There was no response. "Kara! Please, honey, stay awake." Her eyes fluttered as he placed her in the seat. "I'll be back in a sec. Hold on."

On the way to the hospital, he called Jack to tell him what was happening and asked him the let Kara's mother and Paul know. "I don't have their number and don't have time to find it on Kara's phone."

"Don't panic, Kevin. She's been in and out of the hospital many times."

"She was nearly unconscious on the kitchen floor when I got there. I talked to her earlier in the afternoon. She seemed tired. I should have come then. If anything happens to her."

"Kevin! Keep your cool. I'll meet you at the hospital. I'll take care of Jenny and Paul. You just take good care of Kara."

"I'm doing my best. Just hope Betsy doesn't falter or something. So far she's doing well, no radio, just cruising along nicely."

"That's a good thing. How about the pets?"

"I think they're fine for tonight, but you might want to go out tomorrow and feed and water them. I'm sure the doctor will keep Kara, and I want to stay with her."

"I understand. We all know how you feel about her. All of us except you. You need to wake up, boy, and see what a treasure she is."

"Yes, I know she is."

"Well, what took you so long?"

"Slow learner. See you at the hospital."

****

The doctor entered the waiting room and addressed Kevin and Jack. "We've sedated her so she'll be out of it for quite some time. She won't be responsive so there is no need for you to stay. You can go home for now."

"No can do, doctor." Kevin said. "I'm staying with her."

Jack spoke up. "She'll be in good hands with Kevin so I'll leave for now. Her mother and brother will be here in the morning." He turned to Kevin. "See ya, pal."

Kevin rose and gave Jack a brotherly hug. "I'll call if anything new transpires."

After Jack left the room, Kevin asked the doctor, "Have you determined what happened?"

"We don't know for sure, but we suspect one of the stints failed and needs to be replaced. We'll know more later." He looked at his notes. "Are you a relative?"

"No, a close friend...very close. I think she would want to see a familiar face when she wakes up."

"You do what you have to do. I don't want to scare you, but I need to tell you she is in trouble right now. Her heart operates at only twenty to twenty-five percent. I frankly don't know how she does it. I treated Kara when she lived here before and have a few times since she moved back and she's a fighter, but this time..." He shook his head. "We just have to wait and see."

"I understand."

The doctor walked back with Kevin to Kara's room where she was sleeping peacefully and breathing with the help of a respirator. Kevin took her hand and kissed it and held onto it while the doctor checked the machines and her pulse.

After the doctor left, Kevin laid his head down on the edge of the bed. "I love you, Kara. Come back to me." Something suddenly washed over him and he looked up toward the ceiling.

"God? Is that you?" Jenny told him he would be scooped up and taken to higher ground. She was right.

"Dear merciful God, I know I turned my back on You, but I

was told You never turn Your back on anyone, so I hope I'm not too late in accepting You and Your only son Jesus back into my heart. I'm pleading for Your help. We need Your healing hands to touch Kara and guide the doctors to give her what she needs to go on with her task. There is no one who loves You more and who praises Your glory daily. I'm sorry it took this tragedy for me to see how much I need You."

He touched her cheek, then kissed her hand again. "I ask these things of You as Your humble servant. I promise to abide by Your will in everything I say and do. Amen."

He didn't know when he fell asleep with his head on the edge of the bed, but a nurse came in and tapped him on the shoulder. "Here is a pillow. Perhaps you would be more comfortable in the recliner."

He smiled at her. "Thanks, but I'm fine. I want to be right here when she wakes."

The nurse nodded then checked Kara's vitals. "Well, I'll leave the pillow just in case."

He looked at his watch. Two o'clock in the morning. He then pressed his lips to her hand again. "If you can hear me, sweetheart, I love you more than my own life. If I could take your place, I'd do it in a heartbeat. You have so much to give to others."

Jenny and Paul arrived very early the next morning and Kevin offered to step aside so they could hold her hand but Jenny said, "Don't get up, Kevin. I think you're the one she would want to see first."

Kevin looked at her, puzzled.

"She loves you. A mother knows. And you love her. A heart wants what a heart wants."

"Mom," Paul said, letting his breath out in a huff, "do you ever think before you speak."

"Hush up. I'll say what I want to say."

"It's okay," Kevin returned. "She's right, Paul. I love her and I hope she loves me and when she wakes up I would like to ask her to marry me if I can have your blessing...and yours Jenny."

Jenny clapped her hands. "Well, if she doesn't, I will."

Paul slapped his forehead. "Oh, merciful God, please let

Kara say yes. I like Kevin but I don't want him for a step-daddy."

Jenny gave Paul a scathing look. "It was just a figure of speech. Sometimes, Paul, you can be so irritating."

Paul kissed her on the cheek and she quickly wiped it off. "Don't try to butter me up."

They all three sat and prayed their own separate prayers and after they were through, Jenny put her arm around Kevin. "God came, didn't he?"

"Yes, Jenny. I asked Him to come." He smiled at her. "You were right. I got swooped up."

"Oh, boy," Paul interjected, "old Satan is surely quaking in his boots."

Just then the doctor came in. "Hi, Jenny, Paul. Good to see you, but not under these circumstances." He looked at Kara for a long moment. "We are taking her to surgery to repair some damage to two of the stints. It'll be awhile, so why don't you go get something to eat and drink in the cafeteria."

They watched them wheel Kara out of the room, but Kevin refused to go. "I need to visit the men's room then I'll wait here, just in case." He handed Paul his cell. "Here, put your numbers in my phone. If I need you I'll call."

As Paul did so, he said, "We'll bring you something. Sandwich and black coffee okay?"

"Whatever," Kevin said. "I really don't have much of an appetite."

"You have to eat and keep up your strength, Kevin," Jenny urged. "Mother knows best."

Paul shook his head. "Don't argue, Kevin. Just eat what she brings you."

Kevin nodded and called out as they left the room, "Love you, Jenny."

"I know," she called back.

****

Later that evening they brought Kara back to her room. She was still sedated and the doctor said they had done all they could do to repair the damage and hoped it was enough.

"We'll know more tomorrow, but we need to leave her on the respirator for a while longer, at least for a few hours at a time." He looked at Jenny. "We have hospitality rooms where you'd be comfortable. You can come back in the morning."

"Thank you. I think I will take advantage of that," Jenny said.

"Kevin, you and I could share a room," Paul offered.

"I'm staying here. You go on. I'll call if she wakes."

Jenny patted his cheek. "You need rest, my dear."

"I know. I'll rest here. I wouldn't be able to sleep somewhere else."

Paul smiled. "You got it bad. That old love bug done bit you all over."

Jenny huffed and pointed to Paul. "I am only going to say this once. Hush up!"

CHAPTER TWENTY EIGHT

Sunday morning brought sunshine into the room. Kevin stood up to get the kinks out of his back. He looked at Kara still sleeping. His eyes misted. "God loves you and so do I."

The Physician Assistant came into the room and said they needed to take her to x-ray to see if the surgery was doing what it was intended to do.

Kevin took Kara's hand. "I'll be right here when you get back, sweetheart."

Jenny and Paul arrived just as they were taking her out of the room.

"They're going to x-ray to see if everything is okay."

"Did she wake?" Paul asked.

"No, but she doesn't seem to be in any distress. Of course, she's heavily sedated, but she seemed peaceful."

Jenny handed him a cup of coffee and a muffin. "Blueberry, but it won't be as good as mine."

Kevin chuckled. "I'm sure you're right."

They all sat in silence for a long time drinking coffee and eating their muffins. Finally, Kevin spoke. "I know she is in the hands of God, but I can't help but worry. She hated for me to worry."

Jenny rose and came to stand beside him. "I know. That's why we tried never to act worried around her, but inside we felt just like you are feeling now. Just trust in God and the glories only He can bring into our lives."

Kevin rose and embraced Jenny. "I know where Kara gets her strength. You both are amazing women."

Paul snickered. "That will go to Mom's head and we won't be able to live with her."

Jenny whirled around and shook her finger at her son. "One more smart word out of you and you can go to your room."

Later that morning, when they brought Kara back, the doctor stated, "Things look pretty good."

"Praise God," they all three said at the same time.

"We need to keep her sedated a little longer, but we'll wean her off the respirator a little at a time and see how she breathes on her own."

"When will you start that?" Kevin asked.

"Right now as a matter of fact." The doctor unhooked the necessary equipment and stood watch while she breathed in and out. "We'll put it back on in thirty minutes, but if her breathing becomes labored a sensor goes off and we'll hook her right back up."

"Thanks, doctor," Kevin said. Jenny and Paul nodded their thanks.

This went on all afternoon and evening. Respirator on, then off, then on again. It was longer off each time and Kevin watched closely, monitoring her breathing. Jenny and Paul went to get some supper while Kevin stayed, prayed and hoped she would wake soon.

In the wee hours of Monday morning Kevin woke feeling Kara's hand on his cheek. Tears sprang to his eyes when he looked up to see her looking back at him.

"Oh, my darling Kara. You're awake! And breathing on your own. How do you feel?"

"You need a shave."

"That's all you got? I need a shave?" He laughed. "I've been here since Friday going crazy waiting for you to wake up."

"What day is it?"

"Monday."

"You probably need a shower too."

"You're unbelievable." He smiled. "I thought maybe you'd say how much you love me."

"What makes you think I do?"

"Your mother told me."

"She's here?"

"Yes, she and Paul have been here since Saturday morning. I'm getting ready to call them to tell them you are awake, but first there's something I want to ask you. It's what I was going to ask you over Coney dogs Friday night, but you did that scary 'can't breathe' thing." He cleared his throat. "Kara Peters, will you marry me? I've already got blessings from your mom and brother."

"Oh, Kevin, look what you'd be getting yourself into. Hospital visits, farm house, pets, kids, kids, kids." Her voice was weak and her breathing a little labored when she spoke, but she wanted to make her point. "Are you just worried—"

"I love you, Kara, and I don't even want to think of life without you...or Pooch...or Scooter...or Smokey...or any other stray pet you want to give a home to."

"Don't make me laugh, it hurts." She breathed in slowly. "Am I dreaming? You want pets?"

"No, you're not dreaming and I'm not either. In fact, I finally woke up. You made me face things in my life I didn't want to ever face again, but it made me realize it wasn't loving someone that was painful. It was trying not to love that hurt...and I truly, truly love you with all my heart."

"Kevin, I *do* love you. That's why I can't marry you. I don't want to burden you."

"Sweetheart, don't you know one day with you as my wife is worth more to me than a million days without you?"

Just then a nurse poked her head around the door. "Sorry, I didn't mean to eavesdrop but I heard what was going on in here." She cocked her head toward Kara. "If I were you, child, I'd say yes. This man saved your life by getting you here on time and he never left your side. I'd marry him for that reason alone, but the fact that he loves you so much is an even better reason." She shrugged. "Just saying." She stepped aside to let Jenny and Paul in.

Kevin rose and hugged Jenny. "I was just getting ready to call you."

Paul held up his cell. "Been awake for hours. Jack has

called and texted a hundred times even though I told him I'd call if we needed him."

Kevin smiled. "That's Jack...Kara's other mother."

Jenny hurried to Kara's side and kissed her on the cheek, then looked at Kevin. "Did she say yes?"

"No, but everyone else has." He laughed. "So I have other options."

Kara smiled. "Before I agree to marry you, I need to ask you a question." She breathed in and out slowly again. "I may have been delusional, but while I was in a coma, God appeared to me, and I thought I heard you praying."

"You did. God did not forsake me after all. He heard my pleas to bring you back to me."

"Then yes, yes, yes, I will marry you and the sooner the better before those other options come calling."

He turned to Jenny and Paul. "I'm the luckiest man on earth." He kissed Kara on the tip of her nose. "Getting a woman who is not only beautiful and amazing, but can change the oil on the car. What more could a man ask for?"

"You're not lucky. You're crazy," Kara said.

"I have a confession. When Brad told me you were going to sell Betsy, I told him I would buy her. I gave him a few bucks commission for his trouble."

Kara stared at him. "You don't need another car, especially an old one."

"Yeah, I know but..."

They both smiled at that familiar phrase. He took her hand and planted a kiss on the palm. "I couldn't let her go. Remember it was Betsy who brought us together. You had me at 'I kissed the wrong man'. That would have never happened if it hadn't been for Betsy."

"You turned out to be the right man after all."

"Betsy will always be a part of our family. When she has traveled her last mile..." he laughed, "we'll fill her with dirt and use her as a planter in the back yard."

****

Kara recovered quicker than expected. Expected by

everyone except those who knew her well. A few weeks later, the wedding was planned and executed to perfection. Barb was the matron of honor, Jack the best man and Pooch the ring bearer; with Aaron, dressed in the tux Kevin rented for him, as backup in case Pooch decided to make a run for it with the rings attached to his collar. Teresa was flower girl and, though the organist played an appropriate wedding song, Teresa hummed 'Jesus Loves Me' all the way down the aisle while scattering rose petals.

The church overflowed with well-wishers and a lot of children who took advantage of Kids Haven were there as well. Several young people had already taken Jesus as their personal savior and that delighted Kara more than anything...except becoming Mrs. Kevin Michals, without the 'e'. That was without a doubt the happiest she had been in her life.

After the ceremony and reception, they said their goodbyes to Jenny and Paul and the rest of her family who had to go back to Joliet.

Jenny hugged Kara. "I am so happy for you and love you both to the moon and back."

"I'm happy for me, too, and love you more." Kara glanced at her brothers and their families who were beaming from ear to ear. "You too. You're all the best."

Kevin then drove them back to the farm in Betsy who, true to form, rang out with 'Love Me Tender' at top volume.

"Ahhh, just like old times," Kevin remarked as they pulled into the drive. He got out and walked around to the other side. "You know, if you look just right at the bent front bumper, you'd swear this old Buick was smiling."

"I know I am," Kara said, a big grin on her face.

He opened the back door of the car first to let Pooch out, then very gallantly opened the passenger door for his new bride and took her hand. "My lady, we're home."

As they walked toward the house, Kevin's mouth dropped into a sour curve upon discovering he had tread on Pooch's toilet.

"Ohhh, Kevin," Kara moaned, holding her nose but barely able to contain her giggles. "How awful."

"Not at all," he said, calmly wiping his shoe in a clump of

clean grass. "As a matter of fact, everything is normal again...your kind of normal. No," he corrected, "*Our* kind of normal."

EPILOGUE

One of their greatest joys was being God Parents to Crissie, Barb and John's daughter. They loved spoiling her over the years. Crissie thought of them as her other mom and dad and Barb appreciated their love for her daughter.

They got to see Teresa Becker graduate from high school with honors and receive a scholarship for college to become a teacher. Aaron blossomed into a fine young man who took advantage of Kids Haven and helped with younger children in their journey to Christianity. Life for Kara and Kevin had been nothing but magical the entire time. They gave all the praise to God for their twelve enchanted years together and knew with the Lord's guidance, Kevin would continue Kara's dream to make sure every child would be safe and loved.

Old Betsy? She sits in the back yard in the middle of a flower bed as a delightful reminder of the part she played in giving Kara and Kevin the opportunity to know the greatest love two people could ever share. She may be silent these days but her bent front bumper is still smiling.

In Kara's last days, the pets visited her bedside quite often. One day, seeming to sense the time had come, poor old Pooch with his bad hip hobbled to her and would not leave her side. "Sweet fella," Kara said to him patting his head, "I'll miss you too, but we'll be together again someday." Pooch's pitiful whimpering was hard for Kevin to bear with his own heart breaking, but he knew Kara would want her beloved pet with her.

As sad as it was to all her family who gathered around Kara in her last hours, she did not want tears shed. She wanted all who knew her to express joy for the time God gave her and the years with Kevin that made trials and tribulations with her illness seem trivial compared to the happiness they shared.

After the preacher gave the eulogy, Kevin read the letter Kara wrote just before she went to be with the Lord.

Don't cry for me. Rejoice! I've had a glorious life, accomplishing all the things I needed to do for God's glory. I've had unconditional love from my family and a husband whom I've loved from the moment I saw him. He has shared the ups and downs and a multitude of hilarious mishaps with me, making life a complete joy. I hope you have felt my love for all of you in return.

I look forward to seeing you in heaven. I'll tell Jesus to keep the light on for you.

ABOUT THE AUTHOR

Norma Eaton is the author of romance novels, short stories and magazine articles. She was a long time member of Ozarks Romance Authors as well as other writing groups. She and her husband reside in Springfield, Missouri and sing gospel music at various venues in and around the Branson/Springfield area. She values her love of God and family above all else.

www.ingramcontent.com/pod-product-compliance
Lightning Source LLC
Chambersburg PA
CBHW061201170626
46809CB00003B/1200